A shipwreck!

Elizabeth's eyes scanned the ocean floor. Amazing. *There were all sorts of interesting things down here. A piece of sea glass. An empty ink jar. A small length of chain with a sailing clamp on it . . .*

Wham! *It took all Elizabeth's discipline not to gasp and suck water into her lungs. Her hand had just bumped against something hard and crusted with barnacles. Something muddy-colored and almost hidden. Curiously, she reached down and her hand closed over it.*

Immediately, the water around her began to feel cold. Icy cold.

Brrrrr. *Elizabeth tossed the object into her bag and started to swim upward. But a sudden strong current pulled her off course.*

Elizabeth's heart thumped hard and she tried hard not to panic. Sometimes these currents could be stronger than she was. She kicked her legs harder, her fins scraping the silty floor.

The current seemed to wrap itself around her, and turn her over and over in its grasp. As she turned, she watched the powerful current seem to pull the floor of the ocean apart. With each revolution, she caught the glimpse of a mast. A porthole. The caved-in side of a boat.

A shipwreck!

Bantam Books in the SWEET VALLEY TWINS AND FRIENDS series.
Ask your bookseller for the books you have missed.

SWEET VALLEY TWINS
AND FRIENDS
◇ SUPER CHILLER ◇

The Curse of
the Golden
Heart

Written by
Jamie Suzanne

Created by
FRANCINE PASCAL

BANTAM BOOKS
NEW YORK · TORONTO · LONDON · SYDNEY · AUCKLAND

RL 4, 008-012

THE CURSE OF THE GOLDEN HEART
A Bantam Book / June 1994

Sweet Valley High® *and Sweet Valley Twins and Friends*® *are
registered trademarks of Francine Pascal*

Conceived by Francine Pascal

*Produced by Daniel Weiss Associates, Inc.
33 West 17th Street
New York, NY 10011*

Cover art by James Mathewuse

ISBN: 0-553-56403-X

Published simultaneously in the United States and Canada

*Bantam Books are published by Bantam Books, a division of Bantam
Doubleday Dell Publishing Group, Inc. Its trademark, consisting of the
words "Bantam Books" and the portrayal of a rooster, is Registered in
U.S. Patent and Trademark Office and in other countries. Marca
Registrada. Bantam Books, 1540 Broadway, New York, New York 10036.*

PRINTED IN THE UNITED STATES OF AMERICA

OPM   0 9 8 7 6 5 4 3 2 1

To William Benjamin Rubin

One

"Spring break," Steven Wakefield said in a voice of deep satisfaction. "My favorite vacation."

"Why is that?" his sister Jessica asked. She smoothed out her bright purple beach towel and bunched up her T-shirt to put under her head so she could stare out at the colorful waders, swimmers, surfers, and snorkelers that dotted the sparkling blue surface of the ocean.

It was the first day of spring vacation, and Steven, Jessica, and Elizabeth Wakefield and several of their friends were spending the afternoon at Sweet Valley's wide, beautiful beach. Steven sat up and took a Coke out of the ice chest they had packed full of sodas that morning. "It's the best vacation because you don't have to buy presents for anybody. You don't have to pick out a card. You're not expected to spend every single minute of it with your family—"

"Thanks a lot," Elizabeth and Jessica Wakefield both said at the same time, cutting him off.

Steven grinned and his face reddened a little.

Elizabeth and Jessica both began to giggle.

"You know what I mean," he said with an embarrassed smile. "And anyway, last but not least, spring vacation doesn't involve any big meals to get all stressed out about. It's a snack food vacation." He looked over at his friend. "Joe, hand me the tortilla chips, please. I think I'm ready for a gourmet spring vacation lunch."

Joe Howell laughed as he handed Steven the taco chips, the jar of salsa, the chocolate-chip cookies, the cheddar cheese popcorn, and every other kind of junk food that Joe and Steven had insisted on bringing.

"Yuck!" Lila Fowler said, turning up her nose. "That stuff makes you fat and gives you zits."

"Who? Me?" Steven raised his eyebrows in a comic gesture of hurt surprise.

His sisters sprang immediately to his defense. "Steven is not fat," Jessica and Elizabeth said at the same time.

"He doesn't have *that* many zits," Jessica added.

Joe and Elizabeth and Jessica began to giggle helplessly, and Lila rolled her eyes. But pretty soon, even Lila was laughing.

It was impossible not to laugh, because Steven had dropped the tortilla chips and was feeling his tanned and handsome face for nonexistent zits and pinching his narrow, well-muscled waist in a vain effort to find some fat.

It was also funny because Elizabeth and Jessica almost never said the same thing, thought the same thing, or acted the same way—even though the two girls were identical twins.

Jessica and Elizabeth Wakefield were both sixth graders at Sweet Valley Middle School. They both had the same long, thick, sun-streaked blonde hair, the same blue-green eyes framed by long dark lashes, and the same dimple in their left cheek. But it was unusual for the Wakefield twins to say anything in unison, because inside the girls were as different as night and day. They looked alike, but they didn't think alike at all.

Jessica loved excitement and parties and gossip and being a member of the Unicorn Club—a club made up of all the prettiest and most popular girls at Sweet Valley Middle School.

Elizabeth thought the Unicorns were silly and often obnoxious. Her interests were more serious. She liked reading and writing and working on the *Sweet Valley Sixers*, the official sixth-grade newspaper.

Steven Wakefield was their older brother, and he was a freshman at Sweet Valley High. He and Joe Howell were best friends and very serious basketball players.

Elizabeth smiled at the laughing group on the beach and stretched out happily on her beach towel. It was turning out to be a great day at the beach. It was fun having Joe along. And today it was even fun having Lila.

Lila Fowler was Jessica's best friend. She could be big pain sometimes, since she was the daughter of the richest man in town and was spoiled rotten. Still, she could be fun once in a while, and she was on relatively good behavior today. Elizabeth decided it was probably because older guys were there.

Steven lay down again and Joe stretched out on his towel and put a magazine over his face.

"Who wants to go snorkeling?" Jessica asked suddenly.

"Not me," Lila answered quickly. "I just covered myself with this new tanning formula from Europe and it costs a fortune. I don't want to wash it off before it has a chance to work."

Steven just held his stomach and groaned. "I can't go snorkeling yet. I'm too full."

"Joe?" Jessica asked.

Joe's response was a snore from underneath the magazine.

"I'll go," Elizabeth said quickly, grabbing her snorkeling gear.

The sun had gotten very hot and the water was looking more inviting every minute. But as they started toward the water, Jessica grabbed her sister's arm. "Not here. We've snorkled around here hundreds of times. Let's go explore something new."

"OK by me," Elizabeth said quickly. "What did you have in mind?"

Jessica pointed to an area about a mile down the beach, an area full of old run-down shacks, a few bars, some bait shops, and a rickety old pier. That part of the beach was called Pirate's Cove, and it had a bad reputation.

"Why there?" Elizabeth demanded. "It's dangerous. Mom and Dad told us not to go over there."

"It'll be OK if we stick together," Jessica

argued. "Come on, Lizzie," she coaxed. "They don't call it Pirate's Cove for nothing. Maybe there's something in that part of the water besides starfish and coral. Treasure maybe." Jessica's eyes lit up at the thought of doing something forbidden.

Elizabeth hesitated. Her parents probably wouldn't like it. But then again, in the broad daylight it didn't look so dangerous. And why shouldn't they do something a little different? Elizabeth suddenly thought in a rush. Maybe even a tiny bit dangerous? It was her vacation.

"OK," she said finally. "Let's go."

"Wow!" Jessica said as they threaded their way through the various shacks and bait shops of Pirate's Cove. "This place is kind of creepy."

Elizabeth agreed. It was practically deserted, and the air was full of the ominous creaking sound of the rickety pier as it swayed slightly. It was a strange sound, almost like moaning.

Out of the corner of her eye, Elizabeth saw two men come out of one of the bait shacks with fishing poles. They looked as if they were going to go fishing off the pier, and she felt a little better. At least she and Jessica weren't completely alone out here.

"Look," Jessica said, pointing out to sea. "You can see a sandbar. Let's jump in from the end of the pier and head for that. Then we'll snorkel just on the other side. Can you swim that far?"

Elizabeth nodded and adjusted the little net sack she wore around her waist for collecting treasures.

In the year since she'd taken up snorkeling, last spring vacation, she'd put together a beautiful collection of shells. She had also collected a lot of other interesting odds and ends. Things that people had lost while they were out swimming. Or things that had fallen out of their pockets while they were leaning over the rail of a boat. It was part of what made snorkeling fun.

Soon the girls reached the end of the pier. "Stay away from the jetty posts," Elizabeth warned her sister. "There's a lot of undertow around them. And remember," she added, "you keep an eye on me and I'll keep an eye on you."

Jessica nodded, adjusted her mouthpiece, and then jumped into the water as far from the edge of the pier as she could manage.

Elizabeth followed her example, and soon the twins were swimming side by side out toward the sandbar.

*　　*　　*

Wow! Elizabeth thought as she watched the ocean floor on the other side of the sandbar. *It's shallower here than I thought.*

But the sea was constantly shifting, and she knew that by tonight, this part of the ocean floor might be a lot deeper. That's what Elizabeth loved about the water. Aside from the mysterious sea life, plants, and spectacular coral, she was fascinated by the way the sea never stayed the same. It changed from day to day like a person with moods.

With a stab of irritation, she watched Jessica disappear around the edge of a spectacular coral reef. So much for the buddy system. Elizabeth was just debating with herself whether or not to swim after her when something colorful caught her eye. Something brightly colored was rolling across the soft, silty sand of the ocean floor. She reached for it and examined it. It was a broken handle from a cup. But the enamel work on it was interesting. She popped it into her net treasure bag and then swam a few yards to the left, where the water was a little deeper. Something metallic caught her eye. Something half-hidden underneath a billowy sea plant. Elizabeth reached for it.

Darn. It wasn't a doubloon. It was the handle

from somebody's fly-fishing rod. She decided it might come in handy sometime, so she put it into her treasure bag as well.

Her eyes scanned the ocean floor. *Amazing.* There were all sorts of interesting things down here. A piece of sea glass. An empty ink jar. A small length of chain with a sailing clamp on it . . .

Wham! It took all Elizabeth's discipline not to gasp and suck water into her lungs. Her hand had just bumped against something hard and crusted with barnacles. Something muddy-colored and almost hidden. Curiously, she reached down, and her hand closed over it.

Immediately, the water around her began to feel cold. Icy cold.

Brrrrr. Elizabeth tossed the object into her bag and starting to swim upward. But a sudden strong current pulled her off course.

Elizabeth's heart thumped hard and she tried hard not to panic. Sometimes these currents could be stronger than she was. She kicked her legs harder, her fins scraping the silty floor.

The current seemed to wrap itself around her and turn her over and over in its grasp. As she turned, she watched the powerful current seem to pull the floor of the ocean apart. With each revolution, she caught the glimpse of a mast. A porthole. The caved-in side of a boat.

A shipwreck! Could it actually be a shipwreck? Elizabeth wondered frantically. *It might just be a collection of sea rubbish,* she told herself. *But it really could be the remains of a shipwreck.* These waters were full of them, but divers rarely found them.

Just as suddenly as it appeared, the current began to lose strength, the floor of the ocean closed over the wreckage, and everything was gone.

Elizabeth gathered all her strength and kicked, propelling herself out of the grip of the weakening current and toward the surface. She kicked harder and harder, paddling with her arms as fast as she could. Her lungs were close to bursting. When she finally broke the surface, she let out something between a groan and a scream of relief as she gulped in the air.

Yards away, Jessica, who was swimming along the surface, heard her and turned. "What's with you?"

"Wh-what's with *you?*" Elizabeth retorted angrily, trying to catch her breath. "We were supposed to stick together, remember? There was this weird current. I could have used some help."

"Jeez, I'll say," Jessica agreed, swimming as

close as she dared. "Look at that. That's the weirdest current I've ever seen. What's causing it?"

All around Elizabeth, the water had turned choppy and strange. Waves lapped around her shoulders and head, almost as if they were alive and trying to capture her.

"I—I don't know," Elizabeth said breathlessly. "I think I saw part of a shipwreck down there," she continued in a shaking voice. "Then the floor kind of heaved and it was gone."

"Are you kidding? Lizzie, that is *so* cool."

Just then, there was a long, drawn-out wailing sound, so chilling it raised the tiny hairs on the back of Elizabeth's neck. Sometimes the wind sounded almost . . . *human*. Like someone sobbing.

"Did you hear something?" Jessica asked.

"It's just the wind," Elizabeth said in a voice that she hoped sounded confident. But the current was beginning to form a whirlpool, and Elizabeth felt a steady downward tug. "This water is totally weird," Elizabeth panted as she fought the undertow.

"Come over here," Jessica said uneasily.

Elizabeth didn't waste any time. Her experience had shaken her. "Let's go back to the nice part of the beach."

"OK with me," Jessica said. "You lead. This time I'll stay behind you all the way."

It seemed to take forever to reach the rickety ladder that led up to the edge of the pier. But finally they made it, and the girls hurried to climb out of the water.

When Elizabeth reached the top rung, she teetered and gasped in surprise. Standing right there, at the very edge of the pier, was a grizzled middle-aged man in a diving suit. He was staring out at the water where the strange currents and waves were still rippling and lapping and raising a foamy spray.

But as soon as Elizabeth appeared, coming up the ladder, he dragged his eyes from the sea and looked down at her with a riveting gaze.

Elizabeth felt slight butterflies of fear in her stomach. She craned her neck so she could see past him, and she was relieved to see that while they had been snorkeling, several fishermen and sightseers had found their way to the pier.

This guy was scary, but there were plenty of normal-looking people around now.

The man continued to stare, his sandy brows knitting furiously as his eyes darted back and forth between Elizabeth's face and the strange choppiness out in the water.

He made no move to step aside so she could get onto the pier. "Excuse me, sir," she said in as forceful a voice as she could. "You're blocking my way."

The man seemed to rouse himself and mumbled something that might have been an apology as he stepped aside.

Elizabeth pushed off the top rung of the ladder and planted her feet on the boards of the pier.

Then Elizabeth heard the man gasp as Jessica appeared on the pier right behind Elizabeth.

Jessica, unaware of the strange tension that had passed between Elizabeth and the man, gave him a friendly grin. "Better be careful if you're planning to swim," she said with a look at his wetsuit. "There's something weird going on in the water out there."

The man continued to stare and nodded wordlessly. Then he wet his lips and began to mumble something in a hoarse voice. The wind was rising and carried on it a high-pitched sobbing sound.

The man lifted his head and squinted out to sea. He gripped his hands together, as if the sound troubled him.

Once again, the hair on the back of Elizabeth's

neck rose and so did the hair on her arms. It was the wind making that sound, but it was too spooky for words.

So spooky it even seemed to be spooking this spooky guy.

His gaze went back to the sea as a tall and foamy white spray shot up.

"Jessica and Elizabeth Wakefield!" a voice called out.

The girls turned and saw Mr. Walker, one of their neighbors, giving them a friendly wave. He sat on the pier with his fishing pole along with several other fishermen all lined up in a row.

"Hi, Mr. Walker," they both answered, waving back.

"How are they biting?" Jessica asked.

Mr. Walker chuckled. "They're *not*. But I need the practice. I'm going out of town tomorrow for a couple of weeks."

Mr. Wakefield and Mr. Walker were friends, and often they went fishing together on the weekends.

"Where are you going?" Jessica asked.

"Fly fishing in Colorado," he said with relish. Then he gave them a wave and turned back to his rod.

"That's good," Jessica murmured to her sister. "If Mr. Walker is leaving town tomorrow, he won't run into Mom and Dad and tell them he saw us here."

Elizabeth nodded, a little distracted. Seeing Mr. Walker here made Elizabeth feel better about what they had done. If Mr. Walker thought it was OK to fish along this pier, how dangerous could it really be?

Now Pirate's Cove didn't look nearly as scary and seedy as it had before. It looked quaint and old-fashioned. As a matter of fact, it even gave Elizabeth sort of a cozy feeling.

She felt Jessica nudge her and gesture toward the strange man at the end of the pier. "That guy is watching us," Jessica whispered. "What's with him?"

Elizabeth's cozy feelings about the place disappeared. "Mom and Dad were right," Elizabeth whispered back. "There are a lot of seedy characters around this part of the beach. Come on. Let's get out of here."

Elizabeth took Jessica's arm and began walking as fast as she could. She wanted to put as much distance as possible between herself and Pirate's Cove.

Two

Jessica hummed happily to herself as she and Elizabeth made their way down the beach. It would be fun to tell Steven and Lila and Joe about Pirate's Cove. They would think she and Elizabeth were really daring to go swimming over there.

"Let's not say anything about what we just did," Elizabeth said as soon as their little group was in sight.

"About what?" Jessica asked.

"You know, about Pirate's Cove. About what I saw," Elizabeth answered, bending down to examine a shell. "Look at this. It's beautiful. Mother of pearl. And only a tiny little chip on the edge." She put it into her net bag and scanned the beach for another one.

"Are you kidding!" Jessica gasped. "That's the most exciting thing that's happened at this beach all year. You saw a shipwreck."

"I don't know for sure what I saw," Elizabeth argued, straightening up and looking Jessica in the eye. "And you saw how dangerous those waters got. The last thing we want is every kid at school out there poking around trying to find a shipwreck. It would be too easy for somebody to drown out there. Then we'd feel like it was our fault for getting people excited and spreading rumors."

"But it wouldn't be a rumor. It would be true."

"Jessica! Come on. That's not the point. The point is we don't want anybody getting hurt."

Jessica stood on one leg and scratched her mosquito-bitten leg with her other foot. But she didn't say anything.

"Jessica?" Elizabeth prompted.

"I'm thinking. I'm thinking."

Elizabeth stamped her foot. "Please, Jessica. Just use plain old common sense for once."

Jessica shook her head. "Why is it that whenever something interesting happens, you're always trying to make it sound like nothing happened at all?"

"I told you already. Now promise you won't say anything."

Jessica set her mouth in a hard line.

"Jessica," Elizabeth pointed out reasonably, "if you tell everybody, Mom and Dad are bound to find out we were snorkeling off Pirate's Cove."

Darn it. Elizabeth was right. "OK," Jessica said reluctantly. "I'll keep quiet. I guess."

"I spy . . . a sunfish," Amy Sutton said, pointing toward the horizon. "Boy, that sailboat is really way out there. No, wait, it's a catamaran, I think."

"Has anyone ever sailed one of those?" Janet Howell asked.

"I have," Lila responded. "In Acapulco."

Jessica shifted impatiently. No matter what people were talking about, Lila always had something impressive to say.

It was the following day, and a big group of kids had gathered at the beach again. Their colorful blankets and towels were spread out on the sand along with two ice chests and three umbrellas, several bags of food, and a boom box.

Amy Sutton, Elizabeth's best friend after Jessica, and Janet Howell had come out with them, too. Janet was Joe's sister. She was also an eighth grader and the president of the Unicorns. That meant she could be pretty bossy sometimes.

Lila had come out again, but since her tanning

formula hadn't been too effective yesterday, she was wearing a great big hat from one of Sweet Valley's most expensive shops to keep the sun's rays off her face.

The girls were all sitting in the shallow water, letting the waves lap against their toes.

"Boy, this is the life," Amy Sutton said with a sigh. "I could spend my whole life on spring vacation."

Jessica nodded distractedly. For some reason, she was restless. Sitting around on the beach was fun for a while, but how long could you sit around doing nothing? She was ready for something exciting to happen—*to her.*

Elizabeth had had an adventure yesterday. But in her typical Elizabeth way, she'd just acted as if it was no big deal and made Jessica promise not to tell anybody about it.

Jessica dug her toes deep down into the wet sand. There was only one word for what she was feeling, and that was *bored.*

"Hey! Check this out!"

Jessica whipped her head around and saw Joe running toward Steven with a piece of paper in his hand.

"Come on," Amy said. "Let's see what Joe's up to."

The five girls stood up, washed the wet sand off of their legs, and then ran over.

Joe was holding up a flyer. A printed flyer. "Scuba lessons!" Joe read excitedly. "Beginners Welcome. Sign up at Number 1779 Pirate's Cove Beach."

"Wouldn't that be cool, to take scuba lessons?" Steven said.

"I've always wanted to do it," Janet said.

"My father said he would teach me, but he's always busy," Lila said.

"I say let's do it," Joe said. "Let's all go over and sign up right now."

"I don't think I want to," Elizabeth said.

"I do," Jessica said promptly, ignoring the agonized look her sister was giving her. So Elizabeth was a little spooked by Pirate's Cove, Jessica figured. She didn't have to take the lessons if she didn't want to.

But then, it wouldn't be nearly as fun without her sister. Maybe she could cajole Elizabeth into it.

She took Elizabeth's arm and walked her a little distance away. "What are you afraid of?" she whispered. "There will be a whole bunch of us doing it. I mean, it's not like you'd just have me to rely on. That would make anybody nervous."

Elizabeth laughed.

That was a good sign, Jessica noted with

satisfaction. If she could get Elizabeth laughing, getting her own way usually wasn't far behind. "Come on, Lizzie. It'll be so cool to go back after spring vacation and tell everybody we took scuba lessons with some of the high school kids at Pirate's Cove."

Elizabeth looked skeptical.

Jessica shot her a sly look. "And you know me. If I have that to talk about, it won't be as hard for me to keep my promise about the shipwreck."

"Jessica! That's blackmail. Besides, we don't even know if Mom and Dad will let us take scuba diving lessons."

"So?" Jessica shrugged. "We'll sign up today. And if Mom and Dad say no, all we have to do is take our names off the list."

She watched Elizabeth's brow furrow.

"Come on, Lizzie, you can't be *that* spooked about Pirate's Cove. So there's a few weird characters and some strange undertows. Aside from that, what's there to be afraid of?" Jessica turned her palms upward. "Nothing."

"You're sure about the address?" Steven asked uncertainly.

The group was picking their way along the rickety boards and planks that passed for sidewalks in the commercial and residential area of Pirate's Cove. It was only a small area, but it seemed that they had been circling and circling, looking for a shack that said number 1779.

Joe handed Elizabeth the flyer to look at. "Back me up, Elizabeth. Does that say 1779 Pirate's Cove or not? We've looked at every little building around here and there's not one with that number."

Elizabeth looked at the paper and handed it back to Joe. "That's what it says." She looked around her, taking in the seedy-looking shacks and the occasional face that peered at them curiously through windows. She wasn't sure she wanted to pursue this any further.

She studied the little building across the street, which said number 234. It was a small, neatly built white building, and the letters were printed in shiny black paint.

"Yikes!" Elizabeth smothered a little shriek as a large, scary-looking black cat scurried across their path and underneath the walk that led up to the door. "I'm not sure I'd want to take scuba lessons from anybody around here," she said.

Steven pushed his bangs back off of his face as he looked around. "I would," he said. "Some of the characters around here may look a little shady, but they're some of the best seamen and divers in the state of California. There was an article about it in the paper a couple of weeks ago."

"Really?" Lila said. Her own face had been reflecting a little concern.

"Absolutely," Steven said. "I think we're probably going to get some of the best scuba instruction you can find anywhere."

Elizabeth felt the knot in her stomach relax a little. Steven was right. After all, her parents always said the best fish wasn't in the fancy restaurants. The freshest seafood was served in the little places by the water where they put newspaper on the tables and you ate shellfish with your fingers.

It made sense that they would get better scuba instruction from somebody who really made his life on the water than they would by taking lessons from some college kid at the local pool.

"Aha!" Joe said, pointing to a ramshackle building. "There it is."

Elizabeth looked in the direction of Joe's pointing finger and her eyes widened. It was the building she had been looking at. But two seconds ago, she was almost positive, there had been the number 234 over the door. Now the 234 address seemed to be gone and she caught sight of old-fashioned brass numbers to the left of the door that read 1779.

Suddenly she realized the building didn't look very neat at all. It looked weather-beaten and its shutters hung crookedly from their hinges.

I must be going crazy, she thought worriedly. *Either that or I've gotten too much sun.* She put her hands to her eyes and rubbed them. When she looked back at the door, it hadn't changed. The brass numbers still said 1779.

Amy furrowed her brow in concern. "Are you OK?" she asked Elizabeth.

"I'm fine," Elizabeth responded in a faint voice. "It's just that I . . ." She wanted to tell Amy how she had thought she'd seen the number 234 above the door a few seconds ago and now the address was 1779, but she realized that didn't make any sense. If she told Amy something like that, Amy would probably worry and think Elizabeth was having a sunstroke.

Maybe I really am having a sunstroke, Elizabeth thought. Deep down, she was half hoping the scuba lessons wouldn't work out. She could use a few days away from the beach and out of the sun.

"I can't believe it," Joe said with a laugh. "It was right in front of our noses. I'll bet we walked right by it two or three times." He went up to the door and knocked.

"Yes?" answered a gruff voice from inside.

"We're here to ask about the scuba lessons," Joe shouted.

There was a long silence, and then they heard footsteps crossing the wooden floor. The door opened with a creak, and a face peered out.

Elizabeth sucked in her breath with a gasp. It was the man who had been watching her from the edge of the pier. The same spooky man who had seemed so transfixed and fascinated by her and Jessica.

"We're looking for the scuba teacher," Joe said in a nervous voice.

The man stared at them a long, long time. Then he bobbed his head. "That would be me," he said. "I'm Joshua Farrell. What was it ye wanted to learn?"

"To dive," Steven said.

"Are you from England?" Janet asked abruptly.

The man's speech was old-fashioned and heavily accented.

"Nay," the man said. "Originally from a small island off Scotland. But I ran away to sea when I was a boy. And I never saw my home again."

He turned his pale, almost translucent eyes toward Elizabeth, and she found herself shivering.

Three

"I can't believe Mom and Dad are being so cooperative," Jessica said happily as she surveyed the wet-suits, air tanks, and hoses that were laid out across Elizabeth's bed. "I thought for sure when they found out we wanted to take lessons at Pirate's Cove that we'd have to fight them about it."

Elizabeth had been a little surprised herself by her parents' immediate agreement and their generous offer to give them the money to rent the equipment. They even agreed to pay for the lessons. They said it sounded like a good learning experience.

Joshua Farrell had told them they could pay per lesson. He had said that he foresaw some foul-weather days. And since he didn't know how many lessons he would actually be able to conduct, he didn't want to charge them for a whole course.

That suited everybody, and Mr. and Mrs. Wakefield had said it sounded fair to them.

Now it was Saturday, and the girls and Steven had just returned from the Sports Rental Shop with all the stuff they were going to need.

"Lila's Dad is buying her her own equipment," Jessica commented sourly. "That means she'll have her very own wetsuit."

"But that's so silly," Elizabeth said, trying on her own rented wetsuit. "Lila will grow out of it soon. Then she'll have to get a new one."

"I know. But Mr. Fowler feels guilty because he's going out of town for three weeks, and it's his way of making it up to her." Jessica let out a long and envious sigh. "Her wetsuit is going to be purple."

Purple was the official color of the Unicorn Club. All the members tried to wear something purple every day. But only Lila had the money to go all out on things like purple wetsuits. In fact, Lila had a whole section of her closet that was stocked with purple outfits for every occasion.

"I wish I could figure out a way of making

Mom and Dad feel guilty enough to spoil me," she added grumpily.

Elizabeth laughed at her sister. "I feel pretty spoiled by being allowed to take scuba lessons and having Mom and Dad pay for it all."

Jessica was immediately cheered. "You're right. Now listen, let's not let Joe and Steven and Janet tell us what to do every minute of the class just because they're older. They don't know any more about this stuff than we do and—"

There was a knock at the door. "Come in," Elizabeth called out.

She smiled when Mr. Wakefield stepped into the room. "Hi, Dad. We were just talking about how great you and Mom were to rent us the equipment and let us take the lessons."

Mr. Wakefield smiled. "I'm proud of you for wanting to take lessons. I think you're both pretty brave to do it. I don't know if I ever told you, but I tried to take lessons once. One day was all I could stand. Then I had to quit. Too claustrophobic, I guess."

Elizabeth felt a little flutter of nervousness in her stomach. She remembered how trapped and frightened she had felt when she was caught underwater in that strange current.

She forced her fears to the back of her mind. If

she was scuba diving, she would have an air tank. She could encounter all kinds of currents and just enjoy the experience, because she would be able to breathe underwater.

"Want to try it again?" Jessica asked her dad. "You could sign up and take lessons with all of us."

Mr. Wakefield smiled. "I wish I could. But I've got a trial coming up in a couple of weeks and it's going to take all my time to prepare. In fact, I'd better get back down to my den. I've got about ten feet of paperwork to plow through before Monday."

"Thanks again," Elizabeth chirped as he disappeared from the doorway and headed down the stairs.

"Just one more day to wait," Jessica said eagerly. "I never thought I'd say this but . . . *I can't wait for Monday.*" She picked up the box containing her own equipment and disappeared into the bathroom that connected her bedroom with Elizabeth's.

Elizabeth unzipped the wetsuit and sat down at her desk. Why did she have such a bad feeling about these scuba lessons? Why couldn't she shake off her nervousness? Jessica and Steven would be there. Her parents thought everything was fine. So what was she worrying about?

It was stupid. It was time to quit focusing on irrational fears and concentrate on the positive things. She was going to be spending some time with a fun group of people. Learning a new skill. And she would probably wind up collecting a whole lot of interesting things for her treasure chest. That was what she called the big carved box in which she kept all the things she collected from her beach and snorkeling expeditions.

She got the box out of the closet, sat down with it on the bed, and idly flipped open the top. She poked around with her finger at the shells and other odds and ends. Then she let out a little sigh of disappointment. It was all pretty boring stuff. Nothing really special or wonderful. Nothing to make it a spring break to remember.

At the end of each of the last several spring vacations, she'd made a collage out of all the things she had found along the shore and in the water. It would be nice to find something really unusual, she reflected.

She stared down at the things she had found on the ocean floor of Pirate's Cove two days before. The enamel cup handle was interesting. The reel handle was junk, but it would be a funny touch. The piece of chain was nice, and the sailing clamp would lend a nice nautical theme.

She picked up the clumpy object encrusted by rust, ocean rot, and barnacles. It would take a lot of work to clean that off. And it was probably just some old nail or something.

She tossed it toward the wastebasket.

Then she closed the box with a snap.

"Jessica! Elizabeth!" Mrs. Wakefield shouted from downstairs. "The mail is here and there is a letter for each of you."

The twins were in Elizabeth's room playing cards later that afternoon.

"Letters for us!" Elizabeth exclaimed, lifting her eyebrows in surprise. "Come on. Let's go see who they're from."

The girls thundered down the staircase, and their mother absently handed them two identical envelopes before disappearing into the den with a handful of bills and papers.

Their mother was a part-time interior decorator and she was shaking her head over a paper in her hand. "I don't believe it," they heard her mutter angrily. "The Fabric House has raised their prices again!"

The girls were too busy looking at their own letters to pay too much attention.

"Wow!" Jessica breathed, fingering the crackly, brittle paper. "This paper feels old."

Elizabeth nodded. "It's looks like parchment or something," she said. "And it is old. Look how yellowed with age it is."

The two girls looked at each other and exchanged a look of surprise.

"Come on," Jessica said. "Let's open them upstairs. Maybe it's some kind of special promotion or contest."

Jessica loved contests, special offers, and promotions. She was always writing off for entry blanks and contest rules.

"If this is a contest," Elizabeth said, "they really went to a lot of trouble."

Jessica raced up the stairs with Elizabeth at her heels. The minute they reached Elizabeth's room, they shut the door with a bang and Elizabeth dived for her magnifying glass.

"Jessica," she breathed. "Look at this writing. It's so old-fashioned. It's like it's from another century."

Jessica took the magnifying glass from her hand. "And look at the postmark. It's from someplace I never heard of. What does that say?"

Elizabeth peered over her arm. "The letters are so ornate, it's hard to make them out. It looks like . . . C-A-R-L-O-T-T-A. *Carlotta?* Who's Carlotta?"

Jessica shrugged. "Only one way to find out. You open your letter and I'll open mine."

Very carefully, Elizabeth slit the top of the envelope and removed the letter inside.

Jessica did the same and then let out a cry of indignation. "It's a chain letter."

Elizabeth snorted and let the letter drop to the floor. "I should have known. It's some kind of practical joke."

She went over to her bed, where a card game had been in progress, and began to shuffle.

But Jessica was rapidly reading the letter for a second time. She hurried over and clutched Elizabeth's arm. "This sounds serious, Lizzie. Listen." Jessica cleared her throat and began reading it out loud.

"A thief has come and taken something from me. But it is only half of the whole. Where is the other half? Someone knows where it is. But they do not know what it is. Or what it represents. Search, thief. Carlotta commands you to search and find the other half. Inquire of all ye know. Copy this letter and send it to six friends.

Tell them to send it to six friends. Do not rest until the search is complete. Then reunite the two halves. Fail in this errand and ye shall be as cursed as the thief of the sea. Cursed by Carlotta."

Jessica lowered the letter. "What is that supposed to mean?" she demanded. "The letters are identical. Why would we each get such a weird letter?"

Elizabeth rolled her eyes and snatched the letter from Jessica's hand. "It doesn't mean anything. It's a practical joke."

"But it sounds like this Carlotta wants something back. Something we took. I didn't take anything from anybody. Did you?"

Elizabeth rolled her eyes again. "Think, Jess. Somebody saw us snorkeling out at Pirate's Cove—probably somebody from school. They know we like to collect things, so they figure this is probably a really good joke. In fact, I think if you want to know what it means, you'd better ask Steven."

Jessica picked up the letter. "But look at this down at the bottom." She rubbed her thumb over a raised insignia. "It's a C, intertwined with a crown. I guess the C stands for Carlotta," Jessica said. "I think I'll start sending my letters out to-night."

"Wait a minute," Elizabeth said angrily. "You told, didn't you? You told somebody about the shipwreck under Pirate's Cove. And it gave them the idea."

"No!" Jessica shot back. "I didn't. I promised you I wouldn't and I didn't."

"Jess!"

"I didn't," Jessica practically shouted.

"OK, OK," Elizabeth muttered.

"I really didn't. So if I were you, I'd plan on doing what this Carlotta says."

All of a sudden, Elizabeth felt inexplicably angry and upset. "It's a joke, Jessica," she practically shouted. "Can't you see it's just a stupid joke? Don't send any letters. It's a waste of time and you're just playing into somebody's hands by doing it."

Jessica was staring at her, her eyes wide.

Elizabeth was horrified to realize that her hands were shaking and she was close to tears. For some reason, this was rattling her.

Jessica picked up Elizabeth's letter and put it on her desk. "I'll put this here in case you change your mind. In the meantime, I'm not taking any chances. Chain letter curses are nothing to fool around with."

Jessica got up and flounced out of Elizabeth's room.

OK. It's a practical joke, Elizabeth told herself as she began to pace around her room. But maybe there was some practical reason behind it. Maybe she really had found something that somebody wanted. Or half of it, anyway.

She opened her treasure box and spread the contents out on the bed. A cup handle. A length of chain. A sailing clamp. A reel handle. There was something else. Oh, yeah. That nail or whatever it was. It was still in her trash can.

Elizabeth felt pretty sure that whoever sent the letters had seen both her and Jessica get out of the water at Pirate's Cove. Mr. Walker, their neighbor, had even called out their names in a loud voice. So anybody sitting on the pier that afternoon would have been able to figure out who they were. And that person could have gotten their address out of the phone book by looking up their dad.

Someone had seen her get out of the water with the net bag around her waist. Whoever sent the letters probably thought she had found something valuable. But whoever had seen her didn't know which twin she was.

So they had sent a letter to each of them.

But what did the rest of the letter mean?

Elizabeth put everything back in the box.

I'm thinking too much, she told herself. *Letting my imagination run away with me. There's nothing going on here but a practical joke. And if it's not Steven who's behind it, it's Joe.*

Four

◇

"All done," Jessica said, entering Elizabeth's room without knocking the next morning, and waking her up.

"What's all done?" Elizabeth said with a yawn, struggling to sit up.

"My letters," Jessica said. "I'm not taking any chances with some curse. So I've written six letters and I'm hand delivering one to everybody in the Unicorn Club. I wrote a couple of extras just to be on the safe side—I'm sending those to Steven and Joe."

Elizabeth laughed. "Don't expect them to send any out. I have a feeling they're the ones behind the whole thing."

"Well, I sure hope not. A real curse is much

more exciting than being the butt of a practical joke by Steven. The Curse of Carlotta," she said excitedly. "Isn't that kind of romantic?"

"I don't want to be cursed by anybody," Elizabeth said, snuggling back down into her pillows.

"Then give me your letters to mail. Do them really fast and I'll drop them in the mailbox."

"Jessica," Elizabeth said in a very patient voice. "I told you. I'm not writing a dumb chain letter that doesn't even make any sense. It's a waste of everybody's time."

Jessica sighed. "OK, but don't blame me when you're cursed and I'm not."

"But what does it mean?" Ellen Riteman asked for about the fortieth time.

It seemed to be the question on everybody's mind.

"I don't know," Jessica insisted. "All I know is that anybody who fails to send out six letters is going to be cursed."

That was all she had to say. The members of the Unicorn Club immediately bent their heads back over their papers and began to scribble.

The club—minus Kimberly Haver, who'd gone skiing with her family; Mandy Miller, who'd gone camping with her family; and Lila Fowler, who was late—were gathered at Janet Howell's house for an emergency chain-letter meeting. They sat around the Howells' big dining room table with notebooks, envelopes, and pens.

Janet was a great believer in the supernatural, and she had insisted that the club carry on Carlotta's chain letter right away.

Suddenly the doorbell rang.

"I'll get it," Mary Wallace offered. She dropped her pen on the table and hurried to the door.

It was Lila.

"It's about time," Janet commented testily.

"Sorry I'm late," Lila said languidly as she entered the room. "But I had a special Sunday-afternoon appointment with Carlos at La Mer, and you know I couldn't possibly cancel."

Jessica watched Lila run her fingers through her shiny, perfectly cut hair. But for once, she had something more important to worry about than being jealous of Lila. "Here's your letter," Jessica said, shoving Lila's chain letter into her hands. "Better get moving on the six letters you have to write."

Lila read the letter and smiled. "No problem.

I'll just . . ." Then she broke off and her face fell. "Oh, no."

"What's the matter?" several of the girls asked at once.

"I can't send any letters," Lila said. "At least not for a while."

"Why not?" Ellen asked.

"Because my father's secretary is out of town. She handles all my correspondence. Thank-you notes. Invitations. Chain letters. Everything like that."

"You're kidding," Mary said.

Lila shook her head. "No. This will just have to wait till she gets back."

"Don't you think you're taking a pretty big chance?" Jessica asked.

"What chance? That I'll be cursed?" Lila began to laugh. A little silvery laugh. "Oh, puleeeease."

Jessica felt her irritation rising. Lila was making her feel dumb. She hated that. Besides, Jessica felt pretty sure that chain-letter curses were nothing to fool around with.

"Does that mean you don't believe in curses?" Mary asked.

Lila gave her a patronizing smile. "Look, when my dad's secretary gets back, I'll send out some letters, since everybody else is doing it.

But no. I don't believe in curses. Curses are superstitions. The Fowlers didn't get where they are by believing in a lot of silly old superstitions."

Jessica pursed her lips. Wasn't it just like Lila to try to rain on her parade? Here was the most exciting thing that had happened all spring break and Lila was trying to squelch it. Just because she had a purple wetsuit, she thought she was hot stuff.

Well, Lila could do what she wanted. Jessica was playing it safe. And so were the rest of the Unicorns.

"No, I don't believe in curses. I'm not superstitious. And I'm *not* playing into some practical joker's hands by spending hours sending out a bunch of chain letters. Forget it." Elizabeth raised the newspaper to cover her face.

Jessica beat her fist in frustration against the arm of the living room wing chair. She finally exploded. "You are impossible!" She had been trying to talk Elizabeth into sending out her letters all evening.

But Elizabeth wasn't taking this seriously at all. Twenty-four hours had passed, and tomorrow they would start their scuba lessons. If

Elizabeth didn't send the letters tonight, she'd never find time to do it later.

"I'll help you," Jessica said finally.

Elizabeth dropped the paper and stared at her, wide eyed. "What? Jessica Wakefield is actually going to volunteer to do some work?" Elizabeth asked. "Do my ears deceive me?"

"No, they don't," Jessica answered grumpily. "If you want me to, I'll help you. After all, you are my twin. I'd hate for something to happen to you."

Elizabeth smiled. "Gee, Jessica that's really nice. I'm touched."

"Yeah," Jessica said seriously. "Because if something happened to you, who would I get to do my math homework—Ouch!" she cried as Elizabeth threw a pillow at her.

"Forget it," Elizabeth said firmly, trying not to laugh. "I'm not doing it."

Elizabeth picked up her pillow, plumped it up, and then lay her head down on it. She was determined to get a good night's sleep tonight. Tomorrow was the big day and she wanted to be as rested as possible.

She closed her eyes and used her tried-and-true trick for falling asleep. She started counting backward from one hundred.

Somewhere around fifty-nine, she was snoring gently into her pillow.

"Cut the mainsail!" a deep voice thundered in the distance.

"It's too late, sir!" came an echoing cry from somewhere above her head. "We're going down!"

Elizabeth heard a crack of thunder, and lightning lit up the black night sky. She sat up with a jolt and found herself sitting on a hard wooden floor.

She jumped to her feet in confusion and looked around. Where was she? It was a cabin of some sort. A ship's cabin. A single lantern swung dangerously as the ship rolled from side to side.

"Abandon ship!" she heard someone scream in terror.

Elizabeth looked down in horror and saw water seeping into the cabin. The level was rising quickly.

She smelled salt water and felt salty air whipping around her. There was another deafening clap of thunder and a gust of wind, and suddenly the lantern went out.

I've got to get out of here, *Elizabeth thought in a panic. She raced for the door and wrenched it open. It was pitch-black as she felt her way along the short hall. She was down in the hold of a ship. A bolt of lightning illuminated a flight of stairs leading upward to the deck.*

Water was pouring down the stairs, making them slippery and hard to navigate.

With her heart in her throat, Elizabeth managed to find her way up to the deck. All around her she heard the screams of sailors as the ship lurched and many were washed overboard.

Elizabeth reached out and managed to grab a rope and hold on for dear life as the ship swayed and pitched.

The weather was wild and savage. The rain beat down on her head and lightning split the sky. Then suddenly she heard a woman scream. She looked up and saw two men fighting with swords on the tip of the prow.

They were dressed in old-fashioned clothes, and one of them was tall and broad-shouldered, with a red beard. The other was middle aged and grizzled. They swore at each other as they fought.

"Traitor!" cried the man with the red beard. "Traitor! How could I have ever called you friend?"

Lightning lit the rest of the prow and Elizabeth saw a tall, beautiful woman.

"Carlotta!" screamed the man with the red beard. "Go! Save yourself!"

The woman was sobbing. "Not without you!" she shouted.

As Elizabeth watched, a terrible cracking sound

met her ears and the boards of the deck began to split, separating the prow from the rail to which Carlotta clung. The beautiful woman threw back her head and wailed. "Noooooooo!" she cried. "Noooooooo!"

Then the ship gave a tremendous heave and began to sink. Suddenly, Elizabeth was under the water. Her nightgown got tangled around her legs as she tried to swim through the cold black water. Something over her head kept her pinned under. Her lungs were begging for air. She kicked and struggled, but it was no use.

Then, floating past her, with a look of agonizing heartbreak, was the pale, terrified face of the woman she had seen on deck.

Everything went black. Elizabeth gave one final kick and managed to break the surface. She let out a scream of relief as she gulped in the air.

Wham! went the door of Elizabeth's bedroom as Jessica came flying in.

"Elizabeth!" she shouted.

The headboard of Elizabeth's bed shook as Jessica landed on her sister and grabbed her shoulders.

"Wake up!" Elizabeth heard Jessica shout. "Wake up right now!"

"I—I'm awake!" Elizabeth cried, sitting upright,

breathless with fear. "W—where . . . what . . ."

Then she saw Jessica's face, Jessica's embroidered white nightgown covered with eyelet lace, and her own nice, dry blue-and-white bedspread.

Elizabeth let out a long breath. "Thank goodness I'm not on a ship," she said in a shaking voice.

Jessica giggled. "You must have been having some nightmare."

"I was," Elizabeth said. She stood up and went into the bathroom to get a drink of water to calm her nerves. Then she went back into her bedroom and sat down on the bed.

"Well?" Jessica said. "Are you going to tell me about the dream or not?"

"I dreamed about Carlotta," Elizabeth said. Her voice was still a little quavery as she told Jessica about her dream and how terrifyingly real it had felt.

When she had finished, Jessica nodded. "It's the curse," she announced.

"*What?*"

"It's the curse," Jessica repeated. "You didn't send out the letters and Carlotta is mad. That bad dream was a warning."

"Ohhhhhhhh," Elizabeth said irritably. "If that's all you can say, then go back to bed." She punched her pillow several times and then flopped down on it, determinedly pulling the covers up to her chin. "I had a bad dream. It doesn't mean I'm cursed."

Jessica shrugged. "Whatever you say. But I'm going to keep a close eye on you tomorrow." She disappeared into the bathroom on her way back to her own room.

Elizabeth turned over and stared out the window at the moon. Her heartbeat was back to normal now. And her sweating palms were nearly dry.

But she still felt vaguely uneasy.

The dream had been so real. And there was something she hadn't told Jessica. Something strange.

In her dream, the man who had been fighting with the red-bearded man looked exactly like Joshua Farrell.

She flopped over on her back. So what? Real people were always turning up in dreams and playing unlikely roles. Once she had dreamed that her math teacher was the lifeguard at the pool. Instead of swimming laps, he made them sit on the side and recite times tables.

A cloud passed over the moon, casting her bedroom into darkness, and Elizabeth shivered a little. The room was really dark now. As dark as the waters in her dream.

It was a lot easier to believe in curses in the dark, and Elizabeth decided to let her imagination off its customary leash.

Say, for a moment, that she had inadvertently taken something from somebody named Carlotta. What could it possibly have been?

She switched on the light and reached for the treasure box, which she had shoved under the bed. She opened the lid and looked down at the silly collection of junk.

There was nothing there that looked important.

Nothing that looked even *halfway* important.

She shut the box lid with a snap, put the box under the bed, and switched off the light. A bad dream was just a bad dream.

And a practical joke was just a practical joke.

I just wish I understood what this joke was all about, she thought as she fell back to sleep.

Five

◇

"I'm psyched," Joe Howell said.

"Totally psyched," Steven agreed.

Lila and Jessica and Janet sat together at the front of the public bus heading from the Wakefields' neighborhood to the beach. Elizabeth and Amy sat together in a seat across the aisle from Joe and Steven.

The weather was cool, so everybody wore their wetsuits over their bathing suits and carried their tanks and hoses.

"This could get old fast," Lila said, pointing toward her heavy tank. "It would be pretty easy to ruin my nails lugging this stuff around."

Everybody rolled their eyes, and even Lila had

to giggle when she realized how silly she sounded.

"Hey, did you send your letters yet?" Jessica demanded.

"I can't," Lila responded. "My dad's secretary is still out of town."

"What's that got to do with it?" Joe demanded. "Can't you do anything yourself?"

"Did *you* send *your* letters?" Lila countered.

"Of course," Joe answered.

"Me, too," Steven added.

"Oh, come on," Elizabeth said with a skeptical smile. "You two probably started the whole thing."

"We did not!" Steven protested. "Did we, Joe?"

Joe made a motion like somebody crossing his heart. "I swear neither one of us had a thing to do with it—I mean, except to send out six letters." He grinned. "I sent mine to all my friends who hate to write and owe me letters. I figured that would pay them back for being such lousy correspondents."

Everybody laughed as the bus pulled into Pirate's Cove.

Suddenly Elizabeth felt a nervous fluttering in her stomach. Why did she have such a bad feeling about this?

*   *   *

"This is where we were supposed to meet," Joe said, putting his stuff down on the sand.

"So where's our teacher?" Steven asked.

The group had walked out to a spot on the beach not far from the shacks and the pier.

"Maybe he decided he doesn't want to fool with a bunch of kids," Amy said. "He looked like a pretty crusty old salt to me."

"That's the whole point," Steven said. "We want lessons from somebody who's really weathered some rough waters."

Lila looked at her watch. "Well, it doesn't look like we're going to be getting lessons from anybody. Who wants to volunteer to go find our teacher?"

"I'll go," Elizabeth heard herself volunteering. It was the best way she knew to shake, once and for all, the uneasy feelings she still had about her dream and Joshua Farrell.

Elizabeth approached the shack from the side. The shutters of one of the windows were open. Inside, she could see a wetsuited figure moving around, complete with hood and mask.

There he is, Elizabeth thought. *He either overslept or got the time mixed up. I'll just go in and remind him we're here,* she thought as the figure sat down at a battered table with his back to the door.

As Elizabeth came around the corner, she saw that the front door was open, so she stepped inside without knocking. "Mr. Farrell," she said.

There was no response. "Mr. Farrell," she said a little louder, tapping him on the shoulder.

The figure slumped down, fell off the chair, and collapsed on the floor. *"Mr. Farrell!"* she shrieked.

But then she sucked in her breath with a horrified gasp. The wetsuit was empty! There was no one inside. It lay on the floor in a heap.

Elizabeth began to shake from head to toe. She didn't understand. She had seen someone in that suit. Someone walking around the shack and moving. An empty wetsuit didn't do that.

She began backing toward the door when suddenly, a pair of hands settled on her shoulders.

Elizabeth let out an earsplitting shriek, wrenched herself out of the strange grasp, and turned to face . . .

"Mr. Farrell!" she cried in a shaking voice.

Joshua Farrell stood in the doorway, staring at her as if she were crazy.

Elizabeth darted a glance toward the wetsuit

on the floor. She opened her mouth to demand an explanation. Then she shut it with a snap. What could she say that wouldn't make her sound like a crazy person?

He took a step toward her and she involuntarily took a step back.

"Sorry if I frightened you, lass. Are ye ready for ye lessons?"

Ye? Lass? Joshua Farrell's heavily accented speech was peppered with strange, old-fashioned expressions like that. But then he had said he was from a little island off of Scotland. Probably lots of people talked like that where he came from.

"I . . . I . . . guess so," she said. "I was looking for you. We thought maybe you'd forgotten or . . ."

"Nay," he said. "I just wanted to check the map before I settled on a spot for our first outing."

He walked over to the table and rolled up the map. "Shall we go to the beach now?"

Elizabeth nodded and hurried out of the shack and into the sunlight.

It was bright. So bright it made her see spots. And the intense heat made some of the buildings seem to undulate.

It was the sun, she thought. *It made me see things. Next time, I'm going to bring a hat and sunglasses.*

*   *   *

"So now that's all ye'd be needing to know about the equipment," Joshua said finally.

It was two hours later and they were all still on the beach. They had spent the entire time talking about equipment, safety procedures, and what to expect underwater. Joshua had spoken long and knowledgeably about scuba diving.

But more important, he had talked knowledgeably about the sea. He had spoken like somebody who had spent years and years watching the ocean. Sailing in it. Swimming in it. And fishing in it.

"See?" Steven whispered to Elizabeth at one point. "This guy is the original Old Man of the Sea. With him as our guide, I'll bet we see stuff nobody has ever seen before."

Elizabeth nodded. But she didn't care how well Joshua knew the sea. He gave her the creeps. She couldn't help feeling that way.

Behind her, she heard Lila give a little cry of unhappiness. "Oh, no!"

Elizabeth turned. "What's the matter?"

"I lost my watch," Lila said in a stunned voice.

"I thought you said it had the world's best-designed safety catch on it," Jessica said a little sarcastically.

"It does," Lila insisted. "It's the best-designed diving watch in the world. And the most expensive. I can't believe it's gone."

"I can," Jessica said knowingly.

"What do you mean?" Lila demanded.

"You're cursed," Jessica said simply. "You need to send out your chain letters."

Lila glared at her with an irritated expression. "I told you, my father's secretary is on vacation."

"Tell it to the ghost," Joe said, laughing.

"Tell it to Elizabeth," Lila countered. "She won't send out any letters either."

The group began to giggle, and Elizabeth looked up and noticed Joshua staring at her. Staring with the same strange intensity he had on the day he had watched them on the edge of the pier.

When he noticed Elizabeth looking back at him, he quickly turned his attention to the water. "We won't be going out today," he announced suddenly.

There was a group groan of disappointment.

"Water's too choppy," Joshua said, retreating to the taciturn and abrupt way of speaking he had used all during his lecture.

"But we'll be going out tomorrow?" Joe asked anxiously. "Won't we?"

"Aye," Joshua said shortly. Then he turned

and began walking away, back toward the shacks of Pirate's Cove. "*If* the weather's fine," he added over his shoulder.

"Not very polite, is he?" Amy commented when he was out of earshot.

"Does anybody besides me get the impression he doesn't like us?" Janet asked.

"He might not seem very, uh, warm," Steven said. "But something tells me he knows more than we'll learn in one lifetime about the sea."

Elizabeth felt a little tingle of fear race up her spine. There was something chilling about Steven's statement.

How silly, she thought. *Listening to all Jessica's talk about ghosts and curses and chain letters is beginning to get to me. I've got to hang on to my common sense or I'll start acting as nutty as she is.*

Six

◇

Jessica stood in Lila's opulent private bathroom and looked around enviously. Not only did Lila have her own shower, whirlpool bath, and matching lavender monogrammed towels, she actually had a telephone installed next to the bathtub. Along the spacious counter was every kind of hair dryer, curling iron, brush, and makeup aid imaginable.

Sure, she and Elizabeth had a nice bathroom, with mirrored cabinets and bright pink-and-white tile, but it was nothing compared with this.

Sleepovers at Lila's were always fun. And tomorrow, the chauffeur would drive them both to the bus stop to meet Elizabeth and Steven and everybody else in their diving class. It was wonderful being in the middle of so much luxury.

I could live happily in Lila's bathroom for the rest of my life, Jessica was thinking, when a sudden cry from Lila's bedroom got her attention.

She quickly dried her face and pulled on her nightgown. "What's the matter?" she asked, hurrying into Lila's large bedroom.

Lila held up her hands. "I just broke a nail below the quick and it really hurts."

"Where are your nail scissors? Clip what's left of it. Then it won't be as painful."

Lila stood up and began to cross over to her dressing table. But she had gone only a few steps when she stepped on the hem of her robe and went diving forward.

Riiippp! went the fabric of her robe.

"Ouch!" Lila cried as she fell heavily on her arm.

There were some hurried footsteps in the hall and a knock on the door, and then Mrs. Pervis, the Fowlers' live-in housekeeper, stuck her head in the door with a concerned expression on her face. "Lila? I heard a bang up here. Are you OK?"

Lila got painfully to her feet. "I'm OK. I just fell, that's all."

"Again?" Mrs. Pervis asked. She shook her head.

"Again?" Jessica repeated.

"If you keep this up, you're going to give me a heart attack." Mrs. Pervis looked over to Jessica. "She fell down the stairs this morning. And then this afternoon, she skidded on the wet kitchen floor and slid head first into the kitchen cabinets."

"She did?" Jessica said, fixing Lila with an accusing gaze. Mrs. Pervis shook her head. "I guess she's at that awkward age," she muttered as she closed the door, leaving the girls alone.

Lila went over and sat on the bed. She put her head in her hands. "That's it. I really am cursed," she moaned. "I didn't believe it at first. But I fell down the steps, slid in the kitchen, lost my watch, and ripped my favorite robe." She slapped her hands down on her legs. "That does it. I'm sending those letters and I'm sending them tonight."

Jessica breathed a sigh of relief. It seemed that she couldn't talk sense to Elizabeth, but at least Lila was getting the message.

Lila went over to her desk, opened the drawer, and took out several sheets of heavy monogrammed paper. Then she reached for her pen. It was a La Plume fountain pen—the fanciest and most expensive pen on the market.

She opened the top and . . . *Splat*.

Lila let out an enraged scream as a stream of black ink shot out of the pen and hit her squarely in the eye. "That does it!" she said angrily, throwing the pen down.

She stood up and looked toward the ceiling. "Now, you listen to me, you ghost or whatever you are—"

"Her name is Carlotta," Jessica supplied helpfully.

"OK," Lila said. "Listen up, Carlotta. I'm going to send those letters. But you're just going to have to wait until I can get my pen fixed."

Jessica snorted. "Just use another pen."

Lila looked at Jessica in annoyance. "Once you've used a La Plume pen, you just can't bring yourself to write with anything else." She went over to shut the desk drawer. "Ouch!" she yelled, when she shut the drawer on her finger.

Jessica crossed her arms across her chest. "Something tells me Carlotta is not into status pens."

"OK, OK," Lila said grumpily. "I've got another idea." She went over to the telephone and picked it up. "I'll call my dad in Philadelphia and ask him if I can use his computer. Then all I have to do is type the letter in once and the computer will make six copies."

Jessica sat down at the end of the bed while Lila dealt with the hotel operator. Finally, she hung up the phone in disgust. "He's out," she said. "But come on. We'll use it anyway."

"Are you sure it's OK?" Jessica asked uneasily. After all, Mr. Fowler was probably the richest man in town. Fowler Enterprises was huge. There was probably a lot of important stuff on his computer. Maybe it wasn't such a good idea to fool around with it.

"No," Lila replied testily. "It's not OK. But if we're really careful, he'll never know. Besides, he wouldn't want his own daughter to be cursed, would he?"

"There," Lila said in a satisfied voice. "I think I finally got it all written down."

Jessica leaned over Lila's shoulder and her eyes scanned the screen. It had taken a long time, but Lila had finally managed to type the entire text of the letter into the computer. She had even checked the spelling.

"Looks good to me," Jessica said. "But now what?"

Lila frowned. "Hmmmmmm."

Jessica didn't know much about computers, and it looked pretty complicated.

Lila tapped her fingers against her chin and stared quizzically at the keyboard for a moment. "I think you just push this," she said, and pressed a series of keys.

But instead of printing the letter, the computer suddenly went blank.

"What happened?" Jessica cried.

"I don't know," Lila answered, her fingers desperately pressing buttons at random.

The next thing they knew, a directory of files appeared on the screen. Then, one by one, the files began to appear, and disappear. Appear. And disappear. Appear. And disappear.

"What's it doing?" Jessica cried in a panic.

"I don't know," Lila wailed, close to tears. "I don't know how to stop it." She pressed several more buttons, but the files and computer symbols began to appear faster and faster. It was as if the system were eating up all the files in the computer.

In desperation, Lila leaned over, grabbed the cord, and pulled it out of the wall.

There was one little electronic bleep of protest, and then a hum, and the system shut down completely.

Lila flopped back in her father's desk chair and stared at the computer with a horrified expression. "I'm doomed," she said. "Doomed forever. My father is going to be furious."

"It's the curse," Jessica insisted. "There's only one solution."

"What?"

"Write the letters yourself. Just like everybody else. One by one."

Lila stood angrily and wrapped her robe around her. "Are you kidding? I may be cursed, but I'm not crazy. Come on. Let's get some ice cream before we go to bed."

Jessica followed Lila out of Mr. Fowler's office and down the hall toward the kitchen. This was really getting to be ridiculous, she thought gloomily.

Elizabeth stood on the sand, listening to the last few instructions from Joshua Farrell.

"Now, I want the older lads and lasses to buddy with the younger ones," he was saying. "And I want one and all to keep a close eye on the group. No straggling. No going off on your own. Understand?"

Everybody nodded. But when everybody picked a buddy, the number of people was uneven. Much to Elizabeth's chagrin, Joshua picked her as his buddy.

He clapped his hands for their attention. "Follow me. We'll be going in along that section of the beach." He pointed to a section far away from Pirate's Cove and then began walking, trusting the others to fall into step behind him.

Elizabeth hurried to catch up with him. "How come we're not going in over there?" she asked, pointing toward the water and the pier of Pirate's Cove. She had thought for certain that was where he would lead them.

"Most people don't like swimming around there," he responded in a curt voice.

"Why not?" she pressed.

Joshua came to a sudden stop and looked her straight in the eye. Involuntarily, Elizabeth shuddered. His translucent eyes gave her the creeps.

"There are a lot of old pirate legends about Pirate's Cove," he said in his strange way of speaking. He paused for a moment. "And some of them are true."

Elizabeth looked around her in awe. She'd never been down in the water so deep. It was incredibly beautiful.

Several fish fluttered by, their fluted tails brushing against her arms as she continued swimming behind Joshua Farrell. She was a good swimmer, but it was hard getting used to swimming with a heavy tank of oxygen on her back.

She tried to keep her breathing even and regular, as Joshua had instructed. But it was more difficult than she had thought it would be.

I need to rest, she thought.

Joshua was swimming just ahead of her, deliberately moving slowly to accommodate the beginners.

Elizabeth quickened her kick. She'd catch up with him and tap him on the shoulder, then point upward. That's what he had told them to do when they wanted to surface.

She swam faster until she was just even with his shoulder, and then tapped him. He turned his head, and when she looked into the mask, she saw a terrifying sight: there was no face behind the mask.

Involuntarily, Elizabeth let out a scream, and the mouthpiece of her air hose came out of her mouth.

She clutched at the hose, but she couldn't seem to get a grasp on it.

The next thing she knew, she was gasping, sucking water into her lungs and choking.

The tank on her back seemed to weigh a thousand pounds. She couldn't swim. She couldn't breathe. She reached out to clutch the arm of a passing swimmer and then everything went black.

Seven

"Stand back. Stand back!" an irritable voice ordered. "She's coming around now."

"Lizzie," she heard Jessica whisper. "Lizzie, open your eyes. Please?"

It seemed to take all her strength, but Elizabeth managed to open her eyelids. The sudden blast of sunlight in her eyes was painful and she quickly closed them again.

Why am I lying on my back? she wondered. *And what am I doing on the beach?*

The last thing she remembered, she was underwater and . . .

Suddenly, it all came flooding back. The memory of looking into Joshua Farrell's diving mask and realizing he wasn't there. She sat up with a start and let out a little cry. That's when she saw Jessica, Steven, Joe, Lila, Amy, and Janet all gathered around her, their faces white with fear and concern.

Steven let his breath out in a long sigh of relief and put his arm around her. "Thank God! You really gave us a scare there, Shrimp."

Elizabeth looked up and saw Joshua Farrell gazing down at her.

"Aye, she's all right," he said in a gruff tone. "She just lost her head is all. Happens to a lot of first-time divers."

Elizabeth opened her mouth to protest, to accuse him of playing some strange trick on her, to angrily demand an explanation of his empty-mask stunt.

But then she realized it would sound crazy.

"Just relax," Steven said, rubbing the back of her neck. "Joe will call Mom and she'll pick us up."

Elizabeth lay back on the sand and closed her eyes. She didn't want to look at Joshua Farrell anymore.

And she didn't want him looking at her.

Something about the gray, translucent eyes seemed to see right through her.

"What do you mean, *no face?*" Jessica asked in surprise.

"Just exactly that," Elizabeth answered. "There was no face behind the mask. It was like he was the invisible man or something."

Jessica looked skeptical.

It was early that evening, and Elizabeth had debated with herself for several hours whether or not to tell her twin what had happened. She still wasn't sure what to make of it, and she didn't want Jessica to jump to all kinds of crazy conclusions.

As soon as he was sure that she was all right, Joshua had walked off back to his shack, telling them not to come tomorrow if it looked like rain.

Mrs. Wakefield had arrived within minutes, full of concern and worry. At first she had wanted to take Elizabeth to the doctor to make sure everything was OK. But Elizabeth had convinced her that she was fine, that all she needed was some rest and some sleep.

Mrs. Wakefield had driven everyone home and then hustled Elizabeth into the house and up to bed.

Now Jessica sat on the end of it and stared curiously at Elizabeth. "Maybe being that far down underwater made you have a hallucination or something."

Elizabeth pursed her lips in irritation. She had thought Jessica would immediately begin spinning a supernatural explanation of what she had seen. In fact, maybe a tiny part of her had hoped that's what Jessica would do.

For some reason, when Jessica's imagination was running wild, it was easier for Elizabeth to keep hers under control.

But with Jessica determined to be rational, Elizabeth perversely began to wonder if there really was some otherworldly explanation.

She bit her lip, wondering whether or not to tell Jessica about the walking wetsuit she had seen in Joshua Farrell's shack. And the way the numbers on the little house had magically seemed to disappear.

Elizabeth took a deep breath and decided to begin slowly. "Listen, Jess, there's actually more—"

"Jessica! Elizabeth! Steven!" she heard her mother call from downstairs. "Dinnertime."

"If you don't want to go back to scuba class," Mr. Wakefield said to Elizabeth at dinner, "just say the word." He laughed. "Believe me, I'll understand."

"Everybody will," Steven said. "Don't feel like you have to prove anything."

"Steven's right," Mrs. Wakefield said. "You had a very close call today. And in fact, I'm not at all sure I want either of you girls to continue."

"Mom!" Jessica protested immediately. "Just because Elizabeth—"

"Jessica did fine," Steven chimed in. "Don't make her drop out."

Suddenly, *everybody* was talking at once.

Jessica and Steven were eagerly arguing that there wasn't any real danger. And Mrs. Wakefield was pointing out that they really didn't know anything about the Mr. Farrell's credentials.

Mr. Wakefield kept changing his mind out loud.

It was all Elizabeth could do not to giggle. Everything suddenly seemed so normal. The dining room table looked reassuringly the same, with it's cheerful strawberry-colored tablecloth and everybody sitting around it arguing in a loud and happy way.

Jessica was right, she thought. Her eyes and her brain were playing tricks on her. Between the sun and the water, they were making her see things that weren't there and imagine strange things that weren't really happening. The wetsuit. The empty mask. The numbers.

"Excuse me!" she said in mock anger, tapping her water glass with her spoon.

They all suddenly stopped arguing and

turned their attention toward Elizabeth. She cleared her throat. "I just had an accident today. That's all. I'm sure Joshua Farrell is a good teacher. He went over the safety procedures a bunch of times. I just forgot to do what he told us, that's all. So please don't make Jessica drop out. And if it's OK with you guys, I want to finish the course."

"Good for you, Lizzie," Steven said.

Jessica sat back in her seat and smiled.

Mrs. Wakefield bit her lip uncertainly and looked at Mr. Wakefield.

Elizabeth watched her parents hold a silent consultation with their eyes across the table. They seemed to reach a conclusion, and Mr. Wakefield spoke. "You kids go on with the class," he said. "But use good sense. If it doesn't feel safe or you have second thoughts, just climb out of the water and don't worry about being labeled a quitter or chicken or anything like that. OK?"

Three heads nodded.

"Promise you'll do what your father says," Mrs. Wakefield pressed.

"I promise," Elizabeth said solemnly, along with Jessica and Steven.

*   *   *

Jessica and Elizabeth were watching television in the living room after dinner when the doorbell rang.

"I'll get it," Jessica volunteered. She hopped to her feet and ran to the door.

Elizabeth heard the sound of Lila's voice. She was talking rapidly and loudly.

A few moments later, she and Jessica were back in the living room.

Lila's face looked as angry and unhappy as her voice had sounded. Elizabeth turned the TV down. "Is something wrong?" she asked.

"Yeah, you could say that," Lila snapped. "I know one thing for sure. The chain-letter curse is real. Elizabeth, if you haven't sent out your letters, do it. Do it now before it's too late and you wind up cursed like me."

"What happened?" Jessica asked.

"I'm in huge trouble. My dad just called, and guess what. After scuba classes are over, I'm grounded. Grounded! *Me!* Can you believe it?"

"No," both twins said at once.

Elizabeth really couldn't believe it. Lila's dad was notoriously lenient.

"Does it have anything to do with the computer?" Jessica asked, her eyes wide.

"What computer?" Elizabeth asked.

Quickly, Jessica filled her in on the incident with Mr. Fowler's computer.

"And you know what we accidentally did?" Lila said. "We downloaded that letter to every single person in the files of Fowler Enterprises."

"Huh?" both twins said at once.

"Do you know what that means?" Lila said.

Jessica shook her head.

"All those buttons I pushed. Somehow the computer sent out the letter to every client, every vendor, every civic leader, every *everybody* that's ever had anything to do with Fowler Enterprises. Through electronic mail. The letter showed up on hundreds of computer screens all over the country from here to New York."

Jessica whistled. "Wow! We're practically famous."

"My dad is so furious he said he might even stop my allowance next month," Lila wailed. "What can I do? This curse is going to ruin my life."

Elizabeth furrowed her brow. It was a horrible thing to have happen. But in a way, it was kind of funny. She smothered a giggle and it came out like a snort.

But Lila caught it. "It's not funny!" she said angrily to Elizabeth.

"I know. I'm sorry," Elizabeth said quickly. Lila really did seem bent out of shape about being cursed. "But look at it this way, you've done what you're supposed to do. The letter said to send out six letters. But it sounds like you sent out more like six hundred!"

Lila's mouth fell open in surprise. "You're right," she breathed. "You're absolutely right!" She stood up. "I may be in trouble. But at least I'm not cursed. Or if I was, I'm not anymore. Right?"

"Seems that way to me," Elizabeth said sensibly.

"I wish I'd done it sooner," Lila said sadly. "I would have saved myself a lot of trouble. I may not be cursed by Carlotta, but I'm still in trouble with my dad."

Jessica nodded. "See?" she said seriously to her sister. "It's not a good idea to ignore these things. Better get those letters out, Elizabeth. Maybe you were right about what happened today. Maybe it was the curse at work."

Suddenly, with a click she could almost hear, Elizabeth's silliness meter switched on. This whole thing was ridiculous and she'd been letting herself get totally carried away. Jessica and Lila were just being dumb. Elizabeth saw that clearly now.

Lila caught her breath in a terrified gasp. "My gosh!" she exclaimed. "I hadn't even thought of that."

In spite of her determination to ignore the silliness, Lila's frightened voice made Elizabeth's heart give a little thump of fear.

If it's so silly, a little voice in Elizabeth's head was saying, *why am I so scared?*

An hour later, Lila was gone and the TV show Elizabeth had been watching was over. Steven wandered in and plopped down beside her on the sofa. He picked up the clicker and switched it to the weather channel. "It's really windy out tonight. Let's see what the weather report says."

". . . ninety percent chance of rain," the weather lady said just as a tremendous clap of thunder announced the beginning of a storm outside.

Steven clicked off the TV. "Looks like no scuba class tomorrow. I guess that's OK," he added sleepily, stretching his arms high over his head. "I'm bushed."

"Me, too," Elizabeth said.

"Me, three," Jessica said. "I'm going up to bed."

Jessica and Steven got up and led the way out

of the living room, into the front hall, and up the stairs. As Elizabeth walked by, she noticed an envelope had been shoved through the mail slot and was lying on the floor.

She bent over and picked it up. It was a letter. A letter in a parchment envelope. A letter postmarked *Carlotta*.

And it was addressed to her.

Now what? Elizabeth muttered in irritation. She shot a glance up the stairs and saw Jessica disappear into her room. Steven went into his, too, and shut the door.

She opened the letter and read.

"What you took from me must be reunited with its other half. Do not ignore the Curse of Carlotta. Do not ignore the danger all around. Be warned."

Elizabeth ran up the stairs and into her room. "Jessica!" she bellowed. "Stop this stupid stuff right now!"

Jessica appeared at the bathroom door with her toothbrush in her mouth and a look of surprise on her face. "Muyyy phhhshh pmmmmm," Jessica said through her toothbrush and mouthful of toothpaste foam.

"Look at this!" Elizabeth said angrily, holding the letter up so that Jessica could see the spidery handwriting.

Jessica's face paled. "Ommmphh . . . mmmp . . . phhhhh . . . mmyppp," she said.

"What?"

Jessica held up one finger, disappeared, then reappeared without the toothbrush. "I *said* I don't know anything about it. Show me." She hurried forward and took the letter from Elizabeth.

"If you don't know anything about it, then Steven obviously does," Elizabeth insisted. She snatched the letter away from Jessica's hand before she could read it and stomped angrily across the hall.

Bam bam bam! She hammered her fist on his door.

Steven opened the door and peered out.

Elizabeth held up the letter. "Did you send me this?"

Steven squinted, looking at the page. Then he crinkled his face in angry impatience. "Come on, Elizabeth. Enough's enough. Don't bug me anymore with that silly ghost stuff now. I'm tired." And with that, he shut the door with a bang.

"Ohhhhh," Elizabeth said angrily. She pivoted on her heel and went back into her room.

"Wow!" Jessica said, staring at her with big

eyes. "Wait until Lila hears about this."

Elizabeth shot her sister a deadly look, balled the letter up in her fist, and threw it in the trash.

Elizabeth tossed and turned in her bed until late that night. Finally, she sat up in bed.

"OK!" she said out loud. "Let's just assume for a minute that there *is* something spooky going on. Why? What are they talking about? What am I supposed to look for? And what do I have that this Carlotta wants back?"

Eight

◇

Bang! Boom! Crash!

The storm outside was fierce. Elizabeth got up and pulled the curtains over her window. Then she climbed back into her bed and continued pawing through the pile of things spread out on her bedspread. It was almost midnight but she couldn't sleep. Not until she'd come up with some explanation.

Piece by piece, she examined the shells and souvenirs she had collected.

What was it the letter had said? She had half of something. And she was supposed to find the other half. What did that mean? Did it mean half of a shell? That was the only thing in the collection that seemed even remotely connected to the strange riddle. Shells often came in two pieces.

But what could be so important about half of a shell?

And how in the world would a person go about finding the other half of a shell?

It was impossible.

Ridiculous.

And very, very frustrating.

She let out a long sigh and swept her hand over the bedspread pushing everything back into the box. The top fell down with a soft bang, and she leaned over and shoved the box under the bed.

Whatever the answer to the mystery was, she wasn't going to find it tonight.

Elizabeth turned out the light and closed her eyes, determined to relax in spite of the loud crashes of thunder and the driving rain outside. At last she fell into a deep sleep.

The sky was dark. But some of the black clouds were clearing and she could see a few stars winking in the sky through the heavy, wet night.

Elizabeth sat up with a start. She was lying on hard boards. She heard creaking noises and then the sound of water slapping against something hard.

"I'm on a ship!" she exclaimed out loud.

"Hoist the topsail!" *she heard a man shout.*

Elizabeth scrambled to her feet and hid behind a stack of barrels and ropes on the deck of ship.

What am I doing here? *she wondered.*

She peeped over the barrels and saw a surprising sight. A beautiful woman with long, dark hair stood on the deck of the ship with a handsome man with a beard and dark red hair. They were laughing together and smiling. Talking softly like lovers.

Elizabeth felt a little embarrassed watching them. But they were so beautiful and looked so happy that she couldn't drag her eyes away.

As she watched, the man put his arms around the woman and kissed her. A sudden wind lifted the woman's hair and cape and it blew romantically around her.

The sound of a cough behind Elizabeth surprised her and she ducked down again.

"Weather's clear for now," she heard a voice comment from the other side of the deck. "But there's more storm brewing. I can feel it on the wind."

"Aye! But it'll brew for a while. Keep the watch for me," a familiar voice said. "I'll be back."

Elizabeth hurried to the opposite side of the ship and saw a man disappear down a stairway. Something about his build and the way he moved seemed familiar. The other man nodded and then sat down on the top of a barrel and stared out over the sea.

She waited for what seemed like several minutes. The wind whipped around her, making her shiver. Then the man who had been told to keep the watch began to nod sleepily.

Finally, he slumped over and began snoring gently. He was asleep.

"Great," Elizabeth said to herself. "Now I can take a look around."

Then she remembered. She'd been here before. And I've seen that couple before, *she realized. It was in a dream. In a bad dream.* That means I'm dreaming again.

But this dream wasn't bad at all. She was enjoying being on the ship and watching the romantic-looking couple. She wanted to know more about them and about this strange, old-fashioned ship.

Vaguely, she had the feeling that something bad was going to happen. She couldn't remember what, though. But hey, she figured, since it was only a dream, she didn't need to worry.

She crept around the deck, examining the ropes. "Wow. This stuff is interesting," she said out loud.

Since it was a dream, she hoped that nobody could hear her. "It's like I've really traveled back in time," she added. "I hope I remember this when I wake up. It would make a great short story."

A sudden clap of thunder made her jump, and a streak of lightning split the sky. Suddenly, from above, a curtain of rain began to pound down. And the wind began to blow so hard, she had to reach out and grab a rope to steady herself.

In a second, the deck seemed to be alive with men, all of them leaping for ropes and struggling with sails as the big ship listed to one side.

Another crack of lightning lit the night, and Elizabeth saw the handsome, red-bearded man leap to the front of the ship and begin shouting orders.

There was a tremendous thud and the ship shook from stem to stern.

"Where is the bosun?" the red-bearded man yelled over the howl of the storm.

"Below, sir," came an answer from somewhere on deck.

"He's supposed to be on watch!" the woman cried out in an angry voice.

"We've foundered!" someone screamed in a panic. "We're taking in water!"

"Cut the mainsail!" the red-bearded man shouted.

"It's too late, sir. We're going down!"

Elizabeth felt the boards below her feet give a tremendous shudder and heave, and then the ship began to rock.

"Abandon ship!" someone yelled.

That's when she remembered her other dream and what had happened. She had been in a shipwreck. And now she was going to be in it again.

All around her, Elizabeth saw men swept screaming into the surging sea, flailing in the foam.

I want to wake up, *Elizabeth thought in a panic.* Please let me wake up!

She'd never felt so terrified in her life. Never had a dream felt so real. If only she could wake up and get off this ship before . . .

"WE'RE GOING DOWN!" someone shouted again.

Elizabeth let go of the rope and began to run. She didn't know where she was going. All she knew was she had to get away. Get away from this ship.

She made her way to the stairs that led down into the hold. From the light shed by a lantern hanging from the wall, Elizabeth could see a man running up the stairs with his hand on the hilt of his sword. Suddenly, he looked up and their eyes met.

It was Joshua Farrell!

There was something so real about the riveting gaze he gave her that Elizabeth opened her mouth and screamed.

Elizabeth sat up with a startled cry. Her heart was racing and her breath was coming in ragged gasps. She tried to focus on her comfortable, dry bed. Her safe, happy room.

Thank goodness. She was awake and off that terrible ship. Away from the horrible spectacle of drowning sailors and doomed lovers.

Then she heard a huge clap of thunder. Through the curtains, lightning flashed into the room.

This was too much like her dream. She snapped on the lamp and stared at the wall.

There *was* something spooky going on. She couldn't pretend there wasn't anymore. Dreams. Hallucinations. Mysterious letters.

"What does it *mean?*" she wondered out loud. "How does it all fit together? And why *me?*"

Nine

"I'll say there's something spooky going on," Jessica agreed the next morning. "Having practically the same dream twice. That's really weird. I think Carlotta is haunting you."

The two girls were sitting in Elizabeth's room while the rain drizzled away against the window.

It was strange, but now that Jessica had agreed things seemed spooky, Elizabeth was determined to find a rational explanation. "Jessica," she said in a firm voice, "I just want to ask you one more time. Are you sure this chain letter stuff isn't some practical joke that you and Lila cooked up?"

"Would I do something like that?" Jessica asked, looking hurt. She was holding the crumpled letter that Elizabeth had thrown away last night.

"In a second," Elizabeth responded.

Jessica giggled. "You're right. I would do something like that. But in this case, I didn't. And neither did Lila." Jessica flopped down on Elizabeth's bed. "She called me this morning and said she talked her dad out of grounding her. He's going to give her her allowance, too. So you see, once she did what Carlotta told her to, Carlotta called off the curse."

Elizabeth flopped down on the bed beside her twin and thought about this. Darn it. Somehow the lady she saw on the ship didn't look like the cursing type. She seemed proud and a little haughty—but it was intriguing, not threatening.

Hold it. What was she doing? It was a dream, wasn't it? Why was she sitting here thinking about the woman as if she were a real person? Or a real ghost?

She was Elizabeth Wakefield. Good student. Aspiring detective—or at least detective writer. She was usually sensible and down to earth. It just went against her grain to do something as silly as comply with a threatening chain letter.

Sweet Valley was full of pranksters.

It would be just like Steven, or Joe, or even Jessica—no matter what she said—to string her along this far just to see if she would get scared.

Then they would gleefully yell "gotcha," or something like that, when she finally fell for it.

As for the dreams and the hallucinations . . .

Couldn't they just be a combination of sun and imagination? Sometimes having a good imagination wasn't such a great thing. Sometimes it gave you a lot a silly ideas that—

"Did you hear me?" Jessica demanded, poking her arm.

"No," Elizabeth admitted. She gave Jessica a suspicious look. "I was just thinking."

Jessica rolled her eyes. "I *said* Lila is coming over in a little while. She told me she's figured out a way for you to send out the chain letters without having to write them."

"What does that mean?" Elizabeth asked.

"I don't know," Jessica answered. "She said she would explain when she got here."

Elizabeth quickly reconstructed the previous evening in her mind. Her twin had spent the entire evening in the living room with her. Steven had spent most of it in the kitchen working the crossword puzzle with their mom and dad.

Neither one would have had time to leave the letter in the front hall.

Lila had come over, though.

Hmmmmmm.

On the other hand, Lila would never be able to pull off something this elaborate on her own.

But who said she was working alone?

"What's going on?" Steven asked sleepily as he stumbled into the kitchen. He opened the pantry, reached for the cereal, and sat down at the breakfast table. Elizabeth had just finished her own breakfast and was busy trying to finish the crossword puzzle he and their parents had started last night.

"Not much," Elizabeth muttered as she tried to think of a four-letter word for *leftovers*. She was still annoyed at Steven for having been so obnoxious the night before.

"Sleep well?" he asked.

She could tell from his voice that he felt bad about slamming the door in her face and was trying to be nice. But if he wanted her to forgive him, then he could apologize. Or else he could give her some information about the chain-letter prank.

"Not really," she said curtly, reaching for the crossword-puzzle dictionary that lay on the counter.

"You mad at me?" he asked finally.

Elizabeth's eyes searched the page and she cocked her head in surprise. "Orts! What's *orts?*"

she asked, deliberately ignoring his question.

"Leftovers," Steven offered.

"How did you know that?" she demanded.

"Lizzie," he said more insistently, "forget about orts. Are you mad at me? Look, if you are, I'm sorry I was mean to you last night."

She looked up at Steven and had to fight the impulse to smile. He looked so apologetic. But here was her big chance to get to the bottom of things.

"OK," she said flatly, looking back down at the crossword puzzle.

She could feel him shifting uncomfortably in his seat. Steven might tease and provoke his sisters, but he hated to really be on the outs with them—especially Elizabeth, who so rarely got mad.

Crunch crunch crunch. He chewed thoughtfully, obviously trying to think of something that would get a warmer response. "Need any help with the puzzle?" he asked.

Elizabeth tapped the dictionary. "I think I'm getting it."

Steven dropped his spoon with a clatter. "OK! OK! I'm sorry. What do you want me to say?"

"Tell me the truth about the chain letters," she said quickly, looking up.

Steven rolled his eyes. "I don't know anything about the chain letters."

"Promise you didn't put a letter for me in the front hall last night?"

"I promise," he said, holding up his hand. "Whatever weird letters you're getting are probably coming from Jessica. That's more her kind of practical joke than mine."

He was right. Now Elizabeth felt really confused. If it wasn't Jessica or Steven, who else would go to such elaborate lengths to play a joke on her?

No one.

That meant Jessica *had* to be behind it. Jessica and Lila. It just had to be.

"Thanks for coming, but forget it," Elizabeth said to Lila as she came in the door.

Lila dropped her shopping bag and took off her raincoat. "You don't even know what I have in mind," Lila protested. "I'm doing you a favor, Elizabeth. You should be grateful."

"Listen to her," Jessica urged her sister. "She's been cursed herself. It's no fun. If you don't believe it, ask her about all the bad things that happened to her."

Elizabeth rolled her eyes.

"Bad things did happen to me," Lila said. She reached into her shopping bag and pulled out a box. Then she opened the box and took out a brand new tape deck. "And I was lying awake last night, thinking about electronic mail and wishing I'd known more about my dad's computer, when I had this brilliant idea."

She reached into the shopping bag again and pulled out a stack of new, unopened cassettes. "*Audio mail.*"

"Brilliant!" Jessica crowed, catching on immediately.

Elizabeth shook her head in confusion.

"You can *dictate* the letter," Lila explained. "Just read it six times onto six tapes. Then send it to six people."

"Are there six people left on the planet that your dad's computer didn't send it to?" Elizabeth joked.

"Ha ha," Lila responded dryly. Then she looked at Jessica. "She's not going to do it, is she?"

Jessica gave Elizabeth a questioning look.

Elizabeth stubbornly crossed her arms over her chest.

Lila let out a resigned sigh and began to put the cassettes back into her shopping bag.

There was another clap of thunder outside, and Elizabeth immediately remembered her dream. The listing ship. The pounding rain. The cries of the sailors. And Carlotta.

"Wait!" Elizabeth said suddenly.

Lila paused.

Elizabeth knew she had been pretty firm about refusing to *write* any chain letters. But she hadn't said she wouldn't *dictate* any. It was a fine distinction. But she could do it without actually looking as though she was giving in. Do it and still save face.

And maybe if she did, the dreams would stop. "OK, I'll do it," she said quickly, reaching for the tapes.

While Lila plugged the tape deck in, Elizabeth removed the cellophane from one of the tapes. Lila took it from her and put it into the tape deck. "Now," she said, looking at the tape deck. "What next?" She smiled. "I'm not very good at electronic things."

Jessica giggled. "At least this can't connect us with everybody in the files of Fowler Enterprises."

Lila pressed a button and the tape deck began to whir.

"Is it recording?" Jessica asked.

Elizabeth examined it. "No. Lila pushed *play* but she didn't push down *record* at the same time." She reached out to take the tape deck and push the right buttons when a sudden rasping voice appeared on the tape.

The words were hard to make out, but Elizabeth distinctly heard three words.

". . . Curse of Carlotta . . . ," buzzed the tape.

Elizabeth gasped and dropped the tape deck on the floor in astonishment. "How did you do that?" she yelled furiously. "How did you put that voice on the tape?"

Lila stared at her.

"It's you!" Elizabeth shouted. "You started all this stuff, didn't you? I didn't think you could have pulled it off, but you did. It's you and Jessica, or you and Janet, or you and Joe, isn't it?"

But Lila's face looked just as white and shaken as Elizabeth's. And her hands were trembling. "I didn't Elizabeth. You opened that cassette yourself. How c—could I . . ."

Lila wasn't a very good actress. It was clear that she was just as scared and startled as Elizabeth. There was just no way she could put on an act that good.

Elizabeth felt so angry and frustrated and scared, she didn't know what to do. So she picked up her foot and brought it down on the tape.

Then she turned and ran up the stairs to her room.

Ten

"Drop out," Jessica begged.

"No," Elizabeth said firmly. "Maybe it's a prank. Maybe it isn't. But no ghost or practical joke is going to make me back out. I'm mad now," she said.

"Oh, great," Jessica muttered sarcastically.

Elizabeth continued glaring out the window of the bus. "Mad enough to fight back—if I can just think of a way to do it."

It was Thursday, and the two girls were on their way to the beach for scuba class. Jessica had taken Elizabeth's arm and pulled her quickly to the back of the bus so they could sit slightly apart from the others and talk.

"Please drop out," Jessica said again. "I don't

think it's safe. Something or somebody's got it in for you. And after what happened the other day—"

"Let's not talk about it anymore," Elizabeth said. Then she opened her paperback detective novel and brought it close to her face.

Jessica let out a troubled sigh. And Elizabeth called *her* unreasonable. If only Jessica could get it through her stubborn sister's head that something really weird was going on. But Elizabeth wouldn't give up on the idea that there was some logical explanation.

Well, maybe there was some logical explanation.

But until they found one, Jessica was going to keep a very watchful eye on her sister.

"There's a note on the door," Joe said, jogging back to the group assembled on the beach. "It says he's out till after lunch and he'll meet us on the beach at two."

When they'd gotten to the beach, Joshua hadn't been waiting for them. This time, Joe had volunteered to run to the cove area and see if he was in his cabin.

Elizabeth had to bite her lip to keep from asking if he, too, had seen an empty wetsuit walking around. But Joe's face looked relaxed and unconcerned, so Elizabeth figured he hadn't seen anything odd.

Steven looked at his watch. "It's almost noon. Let's eat our own lunches." He pointed toward a clump of palm trees. "That looks like a good picnic spot."

The group moved toward the little oasis and everybody took a seat in the shadows of the trees. Elizabeth pulled her lunch bag out of her backpack and put it down on the sand beside her. It was cool under the trees and she was glad to get out of the fierce glare. But in spite of the shade, the sunlight still dappled the sand in the places where it shone through the palm leaves.

Elizabeth stuffed her scuba mask into her backpack and pulled out her baseball cap and put it on. No more sun hallucinations or whatever they were.

"I brought some gourmet yogurt and a sourdough roll," Lila said prissily. She took a little silver spoon out of her backpack and Joe Howell snorted in disgust.

Elizabeth had a hard time not doing the same. But then she felt bad. Usually, Lila's showing off just made her laugh. Why was she getting so bent out of shape?

Because deep down, she was uneasy. That's why.

Her appetite suddenly disappeared.

"Oh, no," Janet said suddenly, looking into her own backpack. "I forgot to bring my lunch."

"You can have half of mine," Elizabeth and Amy both offered quickly.

"Aren't you hungry?" Elizabeth and Amy both asked each other at the same time.

Everybody began to laugh and Elizabeth's stomach relaxed a little. Laughter always made her feel better.

"We'll all make a donation to the Janet Howell lunch fund," Steven joked. He pulled an apple out of his lunch bag and presented it to Janet.

"Thank you, Steven," she said, smiling graciously as she took it from him.

Elizabeth and Jessica exchanged a quick look and secret smile. Janet had always had kind of a crush on Steven.

"You can have a couple of my cookies," Joe added.

Elizabeth reached into her own bag and pulled out one of the two sandwiches she had brought. She had thought she was going to be really hungry today. "I'll supply the main course," she said, handing Janet a sandwich.

"Thanks, Elizabeth," Janet said. She set the sandwich down beside her and reached down for the apple. "I'll start with the apple," she said, giving Steven a significant look. She lifted her hand to take a big bite of the apple when suddenly Steven reached over and whacked Janet's arm, sending the apple flying.

"Ow!" Janet cried in a startled voice.

Elizabeth gasped. Had her brother lost his mind? He might not like Janet back but . . .

Steven jumped to his feet and pushed Jessica aside.

Jessica looked startled. "*Steven!*" she shouted.

But Steven paid no attention. "Move!" he ordered Jessica and Janet.

The girls exchanged a look.

"I SAID MOVE!" Steven shouted.

His voice was so urgent that both girls immediately jumped to their feet and moved over a few yards.

That's when everybody saw it.

A *scorpion!*

"Omigod!" Janet shrieked.

"Watch it!" Joe yelled.

Everybody screamed at once, and Joe, Amy, and Elizabeth jumped to their feet, too. Steven reached over and stomped on it with his tennis shoe. Pounding it over and over again until he was sure it was dead.

Then he looked at the group with a pale and shaken face. "It was on Janet's arm," he explained. "And I swear it looked like it came off of Elizabeth's sandwich.

He reached down and grabbed Elizabeth's lunch bag. Then he held it far away from his body and the group, and turned it upside down, shaking out the contents.

Everyone involuntarily took a step back and held their breath as they watched nervously.

Another sandwich, a banana, and a small package of cookies fell out of the lunch bag. But no more scorpions.

Steven shook the bag savagely. Nothing came out.

Gingerly, he turned it right side up and looked inside it.

"OK," Elizabeth heard him mutter to himself. He squatted down in the sand and carefully picked up the plastic-wrapped sandwich, the banana, and the cookies. One by one, he turned the items over and examined every inch. Then he put them back in the bag and handed it to Elizabeth. "OK," he said. "It's safe now."

"Why did you think it came out of my

bag?" she asked. "I didn't see anything."

"I did," he said in a perplexed tone. "I saw something dark on the sandwich bag, but I thought it was a shadow." He pointed to the spiky-looking shadows created by the palm leaves. "It must have crawled up Janet's arm when she took it from you."

Elizabeth felt all the color draining from her face. "How would a scorpion get into my lunch bag?" she asked. Her mind was racing. If there was some person behind all these terrible incidents, surely they would never take a joke so far. What kind of horrible person would put a scorpion in a lunch bag? Somebody could have been seriously hurt.

She studied every face in the group. No one there was capable of doing something that awful. So who? What? And why were these things happening?

Amy spoke up quickly. "Sometimes there are lots of scorpions on the beach. Your lunch bag was sitting in the sand on its side. The scorpion probably just crawled in."

Steven nodded. "Probably looking for someplace dark."

Elizabeth felt her shoulders begin to relax. Of course. That made perfect sense.

Janet let out a dramatic groan and then started to sink.

"Oh, no you don't," her brother said quickly. He grabbed her arm and hoisted her to her feet. "No fainting act."

Janet immediately sprang back to life and shot her brother a dirty look. "If you had just come as close to death as I did, you'd be fainting, too."

In spite of the horror of the incident, Elizabeth had to choke back a laugh.

Steven had Amy's lunch bag now and was giving it the same inspection he had given Elizabeth's. One by one, he went through everybody's bag. Finally, he was satisfied. "No scorpions. But I think we should move a few yards down anyway."

The whole group gathered their stuff and moved down the beach toward the next clump of trees.

Elizabeth felt really proud of Steven. He had kept his head and taken charge coolly and efficiently. Stayed calm but cautious.

That's the way I have to be, she thought. *Calm but cautious. Keep my head and don't start thinking silly thoughts.* Thoughts like one about a ghost named Carlotta who had meant that scorpion for her.

She felt Jessica pluck at her sleeve. "Elizabeth," she said in a stricken voice.

"I know. I know. You didn't do it."

"I almost wish I had so that I wouldn't be so scared for you now," Jessica said. "Please don't go in today. Please."

"All right," Joshua Farrell told the group. "Put on yer masks and we'll proceed into the water."

True to the note he had left, Joshua Farrell had turned up promptly at two. But he didn't offer any explanation of why he was late or what he had been doing.

In his strange, abrupt fashion, he just turned up, paired them up, and then signaled for them to follow him toward the water.

Things seemed very normal. Behind them, on the beach, lots of kids were laughing and throwing a Frisbee. The sun was bright and the day was cool and crisp.

But suddenly, Elizabeth just couldn't do it. The dreams. The hallucinations. The incidents.

She got as far as the shore and then backed up. "I don't think I want to go in," she said quickly.

Jessica started toward her, but Elizabeth didn't give her a chance to speak.

She kicked off her flippers and wriggled out of the oxygen tank. Then she turned and began to run. She gracefully scooped up her backpack where it sat under the trees and headed for the bus stop.

"Elizabeth!" Jessica called after her. "Wait!"

But Elizabeth didn't stop. There was a sound on the wind that sounded too eerie and familiar. Something that sounded like a woman crying. Sobbing.

Nobody else seemed to be hearing anything. But Elizabeth heard it. And now she was scared to death.

Eleven

"I don't know if they thought it was weird that you left or not," Jessica said, sitting down on Elizabeth's bed. "I didn't stay for class. I was running behind you, but you didn't stop when I called. I missed the bus you got on, so I got on the next one." Jessica looked at Elizabeth and shook her head. "That was the worst bus ride of my whole life. I mean, I was *worried* about you. There's too much stuff going on and . . ." She sighed. "And I think we need to figure out how to stop it."

Elizabeth was sitting cross-legged on her bed, piles of shells and other things she'd collected spread out before her. As soon as Elizabeth had gotten home, she had run upstairs and grabbed her treasure box. She was determined to figure out what she had that the ghost wanted.

Then Jessica had come running in twenty minutes later, out of breath and full of worry.

Elizabeth was touched by her little speech. And relieved. She was one hundred percent sure now that Jessica was innocent. That meant it was safe to share her thoughts with her. "I'm glad I know we're on the same team now," Elizabeth said. "I need you to help me with this."

"I will," Jessica said. "And the first thing I think you should do is write some letters."

"The first thing we need to do is look at this stuff," Elizabeth corrected. "I have a feeling that the letters probably don't make much difference now. Carlotta didn't say anything about them in her last letter to me. The important thing is this . . . whatever-it-is that's lost. If I can just figure out what I have that somebody or some*thing* wants, and find what it is they want me to find, then maybe they'll leave me alone."

Ding-dong!

Both girls jumped at the sound of the doorbell.

"I'll get it," Elizabeth said.

"I'll come with you."

The girls thundered down the steps, and

Elizabeth opened the door. Standing there was a young man she didn't know.

He smiled politely. "Good afternoon. I called the Fowler residence and a Mrs. Pervis said I should contact one of the Wakefield twins if I wanted more information."

"We're the Wakefield twins," they both said.

The man let out a jovial laugh. A little too jovial. Elizabeth had the feeling it was little forced. "More information about what?" she asked.

The man pulled out a piece of paper and showed it to them. "About this. It's a chain letter that showed up on my computer screen. I work for The Market. We're a food distributor for corporate cafeterias. We service Fowler Enterprises, so I guess that's why we were on the electronic mailing list."

"That went out by accident," Jessica said quickly.

"There are no accidents," the young man said cryptically. His face seemed to darken slightly. "And I really need some information."

Elizabeth felt Jessica nudge her arm, as if to say *careful*.

Elizabeth closed the door slightly so that she could slam it shut if she had to.

She was furious with herself. Why had she

opened the door without asking who was there in the first place? She knew better than that. They both did. Their parents had told them time and time again never to open the door to strangers.

She saw his foot creep slightly forward, ready to block the door if she tried to close it.

"I'm harmless," he said quickly, as if reading her mind. "All I want is some information."

"About what?" Elizabeth asked again. "I don't think either one of us—"

"About this letter," the man said brusquely. "About the Curse of Carlotta. It's very significant in my family."

"Why?" Jessica asked.

"I think I need to show you why," he said. "Would you girls be willing to accompany me to the pier located at the north end of the beach?"

"No," Elizabeth said quickly.

"Elizabeth," Jessica hissed. "Can you hang on a second, sir?" she asked, leading Jessica a few feet into the house. "He knows something we don't know," Jessica whispered. "Tell him we'll *meet* him there."

That was a good idea. Elizabeth walked back to the door.

"We'll meet you there," she said. "When would be a good time?"

"Ten o'clock tomorrow morning?"

"We'll be there," Jessica said.

"See you tomorrow then. By the way, my name is John Filber." He nodded and gave them the same jovial smile. But it still looked fake.

"Something is bothering him," Elizabeth said as she watched him make his way down their walk. "And there's something about him that's bothering me."

"Now if he says or does anything weird, we're out of here," Elizabeth reminded her sister as they stepped off the bus the next morning. "Remember, Mom and Dad would kill us if they knew we were meeting some strange guy on a pier."

"I'll say," Jessica agreed. "I wonder if we should have asked Steven to come with us."

Elizabeth immediately wished they had, too. He might be skeptical and tell them they were being stupid. But he would never let them go into a dangerous situation by themselves if he could help it.

Then she thought better of it. "If Steven knew what we were doing, he wouldn't come with us. He'd put his foot down and tell us not to go."

"You're right," Jessica immediately agreed. "It's better that we didn't tell him."

"I'm not so sure about that," Elizabeth said when she spotted John Filber waving at them from the end of the pier. "But I don't feel like I have a choice anymore. Something scary is going on. And I want it to stop."

Jessica reached down and squeezed her hand. "We'll get to the bottom of this," she said.

Jessica could feel Elizabeth's hand tighten on hers as they walked together down the pier.

"Good morning," John Filber called to them.

"Good morning," they both replied.

"Look down here, and you'll see something surprising," he said. He dropped down on his stomach and hung his head over the edge of the pier.

Jessica saw Elizabeth dart her a look and mouth the words *out of here.* Elizabeth began to back away, but Jessica tightened her grip on Elizabeth's hand. Something important was about to happen. She just knew it.

Elizabeth and Jessica both got on their stomachs and hung their heads over the pier.

"See it?" John Filber asked. Jessica looked down at the water. "No. There. Embedded in the coral under the pier."

Jessica's eyes followed his finger. Sticking up

out of the coral was something metallic that winked in the sun.

"It's been embedded in that spot for over a hundred years," he said. "Two hundred years, maybe."

"What is it?" Elizabeth asked as she sat up.

"I was hoping you could tell me," John Filber replied. He sat up and settled himself comfortably on the edge of the pier. "My father brought me out here and showed it to me. He said his father had done the same. And his grandfather had rowed him out here in a boat before there even was a pier."

"To do what?" Jessica asked.

"To warn us. To warn us that no one in our family could touch that. Anybody in our family who touched it would be cursed by Carlotta."

"Cursed by Carlotta!" they repeated.

"Right. So you can see why I was so intrigued by this letter. I've never really known how much was fact and how much was fiction."

"How much of *what* was fact or fiction?" Elizabeth asked.

"Apparently the curse of Carlotta started with my great-great-great-great-grandfather," he began. "He was a sailor on a ship coming from the South Pacific. It wrecked. He survived the wreck and then lived on in this area for many years until he died. But people say his spirit still walks these beaches because he committed some great crime. Because of the curse of Carlotta, he can't rest until his wrong is righted."

The hair on Jessica's neck began to stand up. "Have you ever seen him?" she asked.

John Filber shook his head. "No. But I have these dreams. Dreams about a shipwreck. And they're so real." He shook his head and laughed at himself. "Sometimes it's like being haunted."

Jessica was shivering now. What he was saying was exactly what Elizabeth had described.

"In my dream," he said, "the ship is wrecked because the bosun who was supposed to be on watch wasn't. There's a couple, a man and a woman, that gets separated in the wreck. And the woman weeps and weeps."

Jessica looked at Elizabeth to see how she was taking it. Her face looked pale with fear and surprise.

"I have those dreams, too," she said softly.

"What do you think they mean?" John Filber asked.

"I don't know," Elizabeth replied softly.

"If you figure it out, give me a call," he said. "Here's my card. Let's keep in touch."

"What do *you* think it means," Jessica asked Elizabeth as they sat on the bus headed for home. Elizabeth hadn't said a word since they left John Filber. In fact, she seemed as if she were a million miles away.

"Elizabeth?" Jessica prompted.

"It's a mystery," Elizabeth said suddenly.

"That's for sure."

"I'm good at mysteries," Elizabeth said. "What we saw today was just another clue. You know what?"

"What?" Jessica searched Elizabeth's face for signs of distress. But Elizabeth didn't look distressed. She looked *interested* now.

"I'm not scared anymore. Because I'm going to solve this mystery."

"Correction," Jessica said. *"We're* going to solve this mystery."

"Sorry," Elizabeth smiled. "You know I'd never leave you out."

"To tell the truth, I'm beginning to think I'd like to be left out of this. But where you go, I go."

Elizabeth smiled. "Then think about this. The whole time we were on that pier—and yesterday too—I kept trying to think who John Filber reminded me of."

"Did you figure out who?"

Elizabeth nodded. "Joshua Farrell."

"You're right!" Jessica exclaimed. "There is a resemblance."

"I think—I *know*—that somehow, he's connected."

"He who?"

"Joshua Farrell. He's all over this mystery. In my dreams. In John Filber's dreams. In John Filber's face."

"So how does he connect with Carlotta?"

"I don't know. But I have a theory. When's the next scuba class?"

"This afternoon," Jessica answered. "And then after class, there's a cookout on the beach. Janet called me about it last night. The cookout was Joe's idea." She gave Elizabeth a serious look. "You're not going under again, are you?"

Elizabeth shook her head. "No. But I'll come to the beach and watch. Then I'll go to the cookout. It's time to see what information we can get from Joshua Farrell."

Twelve

"Here's a great piece," Amy cried happily. She came running over with a big branch of dry driftwood.

"Thanks, Amy," Steven said. He took it from her and added it to the growing pile of wood.

"There's lots more driftwood over behind those trees. And a big log, too," Amy said.

"I'll come with you," Joe offered. "Maybe the two of us can drag that log."

"If you can't, call me," Steven said.

Joe nodded, and he and Amy started toward the trees. Down the beach, Janet, Lila, and Jessica were searching for small pieces of wood to use as kindling.

Elizabeth stood next to Steven, helping to arrange the wood so that it would burn long and evenly. "Steven?" she asked softly.

"Huh?" he replied absently.

"You're not mad at me for not taking the class with you guys, are you?"

Steven sat back on his heels and shook his bangs off his forehead. "No way. I'm proud of you for not taking the class."

"*Huh?*"

"You're thinking for yourself. It's exactly what Mom and Dad told us to do. Maybe this isn't the right time or the right class or the right teacher for you. Or maybe scuba diving's not the sport for you. It doesn't matter. What matters is that you do what *you* feel like doing."

Elizabeth smiled. "You're a great brother, Steven."

He gave an embarrassed snort and turned back to the firewood. "Well," he finally muttered grumpily. "You and Jessica are OK, too." Steven shot a wary look around him. "No more mushy conversations, OK? I don't want a crusty old salt like Joshua hearing me say stuff like that."

They both turned to look at Joshua Farrell, who stood alone, down at the shore, looking out to the sea.

"Does anything about him ever strike you as, well, kind of *strange*?" Elizabeth asked.

"Strange? No. Why?"

"The way his eyes are sort of translucent.

Doesn't that seem a little . . . weird?"

"You're not getting on a ghost kick again, are you?" he asked in a disgusted voice.

Elizabeth didn't answer. She wasn't sure. But she hoped by the end of the night, she would be closer to an explanation.

"And then what happened?" Joe asked excitedly.

"And then the ghost appeared," Joshua said in a low, eerie voice. "And he told the sailor never to try to sail those waters again. The sailor turned his ship around, and then when he looked back—the ghost was gone."

"Wow!" Amy said.

It was nighttime on the beach now. The fire was still crackling and burning. They had finished their hot dogs and now they were sitting around the fire listening to Joshua's stories. For once, he seemed to enjoy being with them. He was even sort of *friendly*.

"Who wants another marshmallow?" Amy asked, loading up a long, thin stick with big marshmallows."

"You can put my name on two of those," Steven said quickly.

"I'll eat one," Lila volunteered.

Elizabeth had a stick, too. "Anybody else want

any? Please say yes because I love cooking marshmallows."

"Yes," Jessica, Joe, and Janet all said.

Elizabeth reached into the bag of marshmallows and put some more on. Then she moved closer to the fire until she was right next to Jessica.

"When are you going to ask him?" Jessica hissed in her ear.

"Now," Elizabeth whispered back. She lifted her head and cleared her throat. "Um, Mr. Farrell, could you tell us the story about the ship that came from the South Pacific?" Elizabeth asked. "The one that wrecked on the reef at Pirate's Cove."

Joshua turned his strange, pale eyes on her. He looked startled. "Which wreck would that be?"

"The one that was wrecked because the bosun who was supposed to be on watch left his post."

Joshua's gray eyes seemed to flicker and then flatten out. Elizabeth held her breath. Would he tell the story she thought he would tell? Or were her detective instincts completely off base?

Joshua turned his gaze back to the fire. He paused for several moments. Then he began to speak in a low voice.

Once there was a young and ferocious pirate. His name was Red Beard. He was the cleverest and most feared pirate that ever sailed the seas.

Feared by the King's merchant ships, that is. Never by his own men. For to them, he was a fair and hearty captain. Not one to be feared, but one to be trusted. And because they trusted him, they obeyed.

He had amassed a huge fortune. And it was said to be buried off the shore in the New World. No one but he, though, knew how to find it. He had a map, it was said. But no one knew for sure.

One fair day, while he was sailing off of an island in the South Pacific, he spied a ship. It sailed under the flag of the governor of the island. "We'll take her, lads," Red Beard cried.

And his pirate ship sailed out to meet the governor's ship.

Amy took two hot and crusty marshmallows off the stick. "Here, Steven," she whispered.

Steven didn't respond, and Amy had to nudge him to remind him to take his marshmallows. Joe, too.

They took them and leaned in closer.

Ssssssttttt!

Elizabeth had been so busy listening that she had forgotten about her own marshmallows. And now they had fallen off the stick and into the fire.

But she didn't care. She was finally getting some answers.

Now she knew who the red-bearded man in her dreams was. But how did Carlotta fit in?

The governor's ship surrendered without a fight. They knew of Red Beard. And they feared to fight him.

Red Beard boarded the ship, and then he saw the most beautiful treasure he had ever seen. And her name was Carlotta.

Carlotta! She felt Jessica's hand close over her arm. And behind her, several voices gasped.

"Carlotta!" Joe exclaimed. "That's the curse that was in the letter."

"Aye! The Curse of Carlotta is known far and wide around these parts," Joshua said. "But we're getting ahead of ourselves."

He settled himself more comfortably and went on with his tale.

Carlotta was the governor's niece. And for her, it was the same as for him. Love at first sight. But Carlotta said she could never be the wife of a thief and a pirate. And Red Beard answered that he was a thief and a pirate no more.

Bravely, he handed his sword to the governor and

surrendered himself and his ship. He asked only that his men be pardoned.

Carlotta pleaded with her uncle, and because of his great affection for her, and his admiration for the handsome pirate, he pardoned Red Beard. He presented him with a gold locket bearing his coat of arms and bade him take his bride and his ship and make his life in the New World. The gold heart was to show all that the governor had pardoned him for the sake of love.

Janet let out a dreamy sigh. "It's so romantic."

"Shhhh," Joe and Steven both said together.

"What did Carlotta look like?" Amy asked.

"She was beautiful. With a pale, pale face and long dark hair."

Elizabeth's scalp prickled and her fingers tingled. She had a feeling he was getting to the part she knew well.

Red Beard and his men set sail for the New World with Carlotta. They would all make new lives there.

During the journey, Red Beard split the heart he'd been given. He gave one half to Carlotta, and the other half he wore around his own neck.

The winds were fair and the seas were following until they reached the reef off of Pirate's Cove. It wasn't called Pirate's Cove then. And there was no Sweet Valley.

"What happened when they got here?" Lila wanted to know.

"She started a chain letter that's still going around," Joe joked, breaking the tension.

Everyone laughed. But their laughter didn't last long.

Elizabeth looked around her. Every face was intent. Interested. Fascinated. After all, they had each received a letter from this Carlotta. Or from someone who said they were Carlotta.

A squall blew in from the north, making the cove hard to navigate. It was a black, stormy night, a night without stars, when the ship struck a reef. The ship was wrecked, and the men were flung in all directions. Red Beard and Carlotta were separated, as were the two sides of the locket. Almost all on board were lost. A few managed to swim to shore. But Red Beard and Carlotta were never seen again.

Joshua's voice trailed off.

"And?" Steven prompted.

"And that's all," Joshua said.

"Elizabeth said something about a bosun," Joe reminded him.

"Yes. The bosun. He left his post. He was supposed to be on watch. But he wasn't."

"Where was he?" Elizabeth asked.

Joshua paused for a long moment. "Down in the hold. Looking for the map to Red Beard's treasure. If it hadn't been for his greed and betrayal, the ship would never have struck the reef. It would have reached the shore. Legend says that the ghost of the bosun can never rest until he has reunited the lovers . . . *by reuniting the heart.*"

There was a rustle and a stir of excitement.

"You mean there really is a treasure?" Joe exclaimed.

"Around here? Has anyone ever looked for it?" Janet was demanding. "You know, people *do* find treasures sometimes—"

"Wouldn't it be fun to—" Amy began.

"I'd give *anything* to find that treasure," Joe was saying.

"Nay, lad," Joshua said sharply. "Only a fool sacrifices love, honor, friendship, and eternal rest for the sake of treasure. And besides," he finished, "it's only a legend."

Everyone groaned.

"Why is it that all good stories turn out to be fairy tales?" Joe asked in frustration.

"Well," Janet said to Jessica in a voice heavy with disgust. "I'd say that pretty much proves that the chain letter was a hoax. If there was a Carlotta, she's been dead for over two hundred years. She sure couldn't send out any chain letters."

"I don't know," Lila said. "When I thought I was cursed by Carlotta, I had an awful lot of bad luck."

"Self-fulfilling prophecy," Joe said knowingly. "You expected to have bad luck, so you did."

Lila frowned. "But then there was that growling voice on the tape."

Quickly, she filled the group in on the incident with the tape deck.

"Sometimes cassettes have a loud hum and it sounds like a growling voice," Steven said.

Lila nodded. "You're right. I think I let Jessica talk me into hearing something that really wasn't there."

"Hey!" Jessica responded promptly. "I heard the tape, too. And it wasn't any hum!"

"Yeah, sure," several voices teased.

"It *wasn't*," Jessica insisted.

Elizabeth didn't say a word. She had too much to think about. And she seemed to be the only one who had noticed that while they sat and talked and laughed and argued, Joshua Farrell had gotten to his feet and disappeared into the shadows of the night.

Thirteen

"Good night!" Joe and Janet shouted. They waved as they entered the front door of their house.

After the cookout, the whole group had taken the bus back to their neighborhood. Mr. Wakefield had met them at the bus stop with the family van and had driven everybody home.

"You kids have a good time?" their dad asked as they pulled into their street.

"I had a great time," Steven said through a yawn. "What about you two?"

In the back seat, the twins exchanged a look. It was a look that said . . . *My room. Be there.*

Steven didn't wait for an answer and began yawning again. "Man, am I sleepy!"

Mr. Wakefield laughed. "Try to stay awake two minutes longer, would you, Steven? I don't want to have to carry you into the house."

"So what did you think?" Jessica asked as soon as they were home and safely secreted in Elizabeth's room.

"Now I know what the dreams are about. I've been a part of that story. The story of Red Beard and Carlotta. And so has that guy John Filber. All the details matched up."

Jessica sat down on Elizabeth's bed and looked perplexed. "But why? And how?"

Elizabeth sat down beside Jessica on the bed. "Do you want my *rational* explanation? Or my *supernatural* explanation?"

"You mean you've got one of each?"

Elizabeth nodded. "Let's say it is an old legend. Maybe it's a story that goes around every few years. Maybe it's a story I've heard and forgotten. And when the chain letter came, it made me remember and I began to dream about it. And maybe the same thing happened to John Filber—especially if he's got some old family story that backs it up. And maybe he's somehow related to Joshua Farrell. Some kind of distant relation. That would explain everybody having the same set of ideas."

"That sounds logical," Jessica said. "But there are a lot of things it doesn't explain. What's your supernatural explanation?"

"I guess that I've been cursed by Carlotta."

"Wow! I never thought I'd hear you say it. So you're finally ready to write those letters." Jessica grabbed a tablet and pen from Elizabeth's desk. "I'll write three of them and you write three of them. We'll be done in no time."

Elizabeth smiled and paced the floor like her favorite fictional detective, Amanda Howard.

"I'm not cursed because I didn't send out some letter. I'm cursed because Carlotta thinks I've got something that belongs to her. Or half of it. That's what the last letter was about. Remember?"

"What could it be?"

Elizabeth reached under the bed for her treasure box and dumped it upside down. "Whatever it is, it's in here. I've looked through it a whole bunch of times, but maybe I'm missing something. Help me, OK? Look for a map. Or maybe . . ."

She seized the enamel cup handle. It was old-fashioned. Maybe the little crackly lines on it meant something. Maybe it was a map disguised as a cup handle. She turned it over again in her hand.

Nope. It was just a cup handle.

Twenty minutes later, the twins were still stumped. "I can't believe Carlotta wants any of this junk back," Jessica said sourly.

"I can't either," Elizabeth agreed. "And if she thinks I've got her half of the locket, well, she's wrong. I don't. Maybe she's got us confused," Elizabeth said. "What have you got in your collection?"

"Just a few shells," Jessica said.

"Nothing else?"

"Nothing," Jessica repeated. "I haven't been as good a collector this vacation as you've been."

"Hmmmm," Elizabeth said. She lifted her thumb and forefinger and held them about an inch apart. "I feel this close to putting all these pieces together. There's something I'm overlooking."

She went to the wastebasket and dug out the envelopes and letters from Carlotta that she had crumpled there. Then she smoothed them out on the bed.

"What are you looking for?" Jessica asked.

"I'm not sure. But wait a minute! Look at

the date of the postmark. I didn't notice that before."

Jessica whistled in surprise. "Seventeen seventy-nine. The same year as the shipwreck."

"And the same as the address on Joshua Farrell's shack."

"Does that tell you anything?"

Elizabeth shook her head in frustration. "It should. But it doesn't."

She began putting things back in the box. "I think at this point I'm just going to have to wait for another clue from Carlotta."

"Think she'll be in touch soon?" Jessica asked.

"She's not shy," Elizabeth said with a grin.

"Want me to sleep in here with you tonight?"

Elizabeth smiled. "That's sweet. But I'll be OK on my own."

"You're sure?"

"I'm sure. But thanks."

Jessica stood up and yawned. "Even with all the weirdness, it was a fun night, wasn't it?"

Elizabeth nodded. "It sure was. For the first time, I found myself actually starting to *like* Joshua Farrell. And he seemed to be starting to like us."

"I still wouldn't go back to class if I were you," Jessica said.

"I'm not," Elizabeth assured her. "Tomorrow, while you're in class, I'm going to hang out in the living room with a stack of Amanda Howard detective novels. Maybe I'll get inspired and make a breakthrough."

"The thief rifled the drawers of the desk. The key was there. It had to be."

Elizabeth took a sip of her soda and turned the page of her Amanda Howard mystery novel.

"It was just—"

Creak. Bam!

Elizabeth jumped up at the sound of something being dropped through the mail slot. She ran into the front hall and saw the mail lying scattered on the floor.

She bent down and quickly pawed through it. Aha! There was an old yellowed parchment envelope. Carlotta hadn't wasted any time getting back in touch.

She put the rest of the mail on the table in the hall and opened the envelope.

"The little girl fears the sea, but she has a brave heart and does not fear the curse of Carlotta. The time for threats has passed. Now Carlotta offers treasure. Reunite one broken and sorrowful heart

before the fall of a night without stars, and ye shall be rewarded beyond your dreams."

Elizabeth's face broke into a slow smile. It looked as though she had finally earned Carlotta's respect. Carlotta was trying to get on her good side now.

Maybe she was on the right track. Elizabeth had always heard that you caught more flies with honey then you did with vinegar. And Carlotta seemed to think she'd catch more flies with treasure.

"What's a night without stars?" Jessica demanded eagerly.

"I bet it's a stormy night, where the clouds cover the stars," Elizabeth explained. "How was class?"

"We didn't have it," Jessica said. "Joshua didn't show up. So we just all went swimming for a couple of hours and then we came back."

"He didn't show up?" Elizabeth asked.

"No," Jessica said absently, her eyes still scanning the letter. "He left a note on the door of his shack saying he had some business to take care of and he probably wouldn't be able to give us any more classes. Boy. He sure is unreliable. You'd think he'd call somebody in to substitute or something."

"He doesn't have a phone," Elizabeth said, remembering the inside of his rustic shack.

"Anyway, who cares?" Jessica said impatiently. "This letter is what's important." She held up the page and tapped it with a loud rattle. "Treasure," she said with relish. "Oh, Lizzie, I hope it's not just some hoax. Wouldn't it be wonderful if we could find Red Beard's treasure?"

"It would. But I don't think we will."

"Why not? You've got as many brains as Amanda Howard. She always figures out the mystery. So will you."

"It's not that big a mystery anymore. What Carlotta wants me to do is reunite the two sides of the golden heart. She thinks I have half of the locket. But I don't, so how can I—"

"Hand me the trash can, will you?" Steven interrupted.

He had just come downstairs, still wearing his bathing suit and Hawaiian shirt, carrying a large plastic bag full of trash. One of his chores was to empty all the trash cans in the house.

"I got the trash in your room, Elizabeth. Yours, too, Jessica."

Jessica handed him the little wicker trash can

from the corner, and he began to dump it into his trash bag.

When he was finished, he reached into his pocket and pulled something out. "I found this in your trash can, Elizabeth. Could you guys please wrap stuff like this up before you throw it away? It's so sharp it started to tear the bag open."

He held out his hand and Elizabeth stared at the object in his palm. It was the barnacle-encrusted nail she had thrown away. "No!" she cried suddenly.

Steven blinked in surprise.

"Don't throw that away!" Elizabeth had an idea. She grabbed the object from Steven's palm and examined it.

Maybe it wasn't a nail after all.

She jumped up and ran toward the stairs.

"Where are you going?" Jessica called out after her.

"Meet me upstairs. Both of you," she shouted. Her heart was beating fast with excitement. If her hunch was right, she was on the road to reuniting Red Beard and Carlotta, and discovering a treasure worth more than she could imagine.

Fourteen

◇

"Would somebody please tell me what this is all about?" Steven said for about the tenth time.

"Shhh," both of his sisters said quickly.

Elizabeth scraped away at the object with her pocket knife. The barnacles were starting to come off now.

"Careful," Jessica warned as the knife slipped a little.

Elizabeth forced her shaking hands to be steady and began scraping again.

The three of them were in Elizabeth's room, sitting on her bed. Though Steven had resisted joining them at first, Jessica had grabbed his hand and pulled him up the stairs. "It's an adventure," she had insisted. "And believe me, you'll want in when you hear."

Steven still looked skeptical. "I wish you two would tell me what's going on and quit fooling around with that crusty old—" He broke off in surprise as a small piece of the hard shell fell away to reveal a little, glinting piece of metal.

Elizabeth held it up to Jessica. "Look familiar?"

Jessica squinted at the object in Elizabeth's hand. "If those barnacles were pink and white, it would look just like that little piece of metal in the reef."

"That's right. And if I'm right . . ." She began scraping again. A little at a time. A little at a time. Then finally . . .

"Ahhh," she breathed as the last bit of crust fell away. She lifted something out of the rubble in her palm and held it up.

Both Steven and Jessica stared at it in awe.

"Is it . . . ?" Jessica whispered.

Elizabeth nodded. "It's half of a golden heart. Half of a gold, heart-shaped locket. Carlotta's half, I guess. That's why she's been visiting me. She knew I had it all along. She knew and I didn't."

Steven was frowning at both his sisters. "Are

you two playing some kind of trick on me?"

"No!" they both insisted.

He gave them a skeptical look. "Are you sure? I mean, last night, Elizabeth was the one who asked Joshua to tell that story—like she had heard it before. Then today you guys suddenly produce a prop from the story and—"

"Oh, wow!" Elizabeth cried, cutting him off.

Jessica and Steven immediately leaned over to examine the half heart more closely. Elizabeth had turned it over and was looking at the back. "Look at this!" she cried. "Know what it is?"

Steven slowly picked it up and stared at it for a long time. "Got a magnifying glass?" he asked.

Jessica ran over to Elizabeth's desk and grabbed her magnifying glass. "Here."

All three stared at it.

"*A map!*" they all said at once.

"Half of a map," Elizabeth corrected.

Steven sat down slowly, as if he were stunned. "I think you two better tell me everything."

"You did *what?*" Steven demanded in an outraged voice several minutes later. "If you two don't know better than to go off with some strange guy somewhere, I'm telling Mom and Dad. They need to ground you guys or something."

Jessica put her hands on her hips. Sometimes Steven got really carried away with this older-brother stuff. "We met him there," Jessica reassured him. "And he turned out to be OK. It's just that one of his ancestors did something wrong."

"That's not the point, dimwit," he said angrily.

Jessica could feel the color rush angrily to her face. Steven was making her so mad she was having a hard time keeping the story straight.

"We know we should never have done it, and we'll never do it again," Elizabeth said quickly.

"*I* wouldn't do something like that," Steven said. "And I'm older, bigger, and a boy."

"And neither would we if we hadn't been so spooked," Jessica said.

Elizabeth had told him how the water had become so strangely cold and rough on the day she had found the barnacle-encrusted heart. And how when the letters came, she had had no idea what Carlotta was talking about. She'd even told him all about her dreams and the shipwreck.

Why all the chain letters? Steven had wondered.

Elizabeth had a theory about that, too. Carlotta had known that if she threw out a wide enough net, it would turn up the other half of the heart. And the other half of the heart, Elizabeth believed, was embedded in the coral reef they had visited with John Filber. If she was right, the other half of the treasure map was there, too.

Red Beard had given half of the map, and half of his treasure, to his bride. If they could figure out some way to dig it out of the reef, they would have the whole heart. And the whole map.

"So the map the bosun was looking for the night of the shipwreck wasn't down in the hold," Steven said.

"That's right," Elizabeth answered. "It was hanging around their necks."

"This is so amazing," Jessica said, her eyes wide.

"So what do we do now?" Steven asked.

"Check the weather for the next few days and wait for a night without stars," Elizabeth answered. "Is the morning paper in that trash bag?"

Steven rustled around until he found the newspaper. Then he located the weather listings. "Clear and sunny for the next few days," he said. "We've got some time, it looks like."

Jessica smiled. Steven was into it now. Really into it. She could tell.

"We could ride our bikes out there," he was musing. "And I could take a hammer and . . .

Hey! Wait a second. Didn't you say that anybody who touched the heart would be cursed?"

"No, Jessica," said quickly. "We can touch it. John Filber can't. No one in his family can."

"Why is that again?"

Jessica shrugged.

"Don't you know?" Elizabeth asked.

Jessica closed her eyes and thought and thought. Suddenly the light dawned. "Because his great-great-great-grandfather . . . *was the bosun who caused the wreck!*" she cried out.

"Right," Elizabeth said with a nod.

"Good thinking, Jess," Steven said. "You were way ahead of me on that one. It's all making more and more sense now." Suddenly he gave himself a shake. "Wait a minute. What am I talking about? This doesn't make any sense at all! I can't believe you two have actually got me believing all this stuff." He smiled. "But I do kind of hope it turns out to be true."

Jessica sat down next to Steven. "Just think. If we find the treasure, I'll have as much money as Lila Fowler. More maybe."

"I'll get a new bike," Steven said. "And a bunch of CDs. And maybe some camping gear."

"I'll buy a purple wetsuit," Jessica said gleefully.

"I'll buy Mom and Dad a mansion in Hollywood," Steven said, trying to top her.

"I'll buy Dad a Rolls-Royce to drive us all around in on Sundays," Jessica said, giggling.

Steven was stumped for a minute. "I'll buy . . . the Los Angeles Rams."

"We'll have box seats for every game," Jessica said happily. "And all the hot dogs and Cracker Jacks we want."

That's when Jessica noticed that Elizabeth wasn't taking part in their conversation. She still looked lost in thought.

"What's up, Elizabeth?" she asked. "Aren't you happy that we're going to be rich."

Elizabeth smiled. "I am happy. But I'm not so sure about the rich part."

Steven groaned. "First you say it's all true. Then you say you don't know about the rich part. Don't you think there really is a treasure?"

"Oh, I think there's a treasure, all right," she said. "But we don't know yet if we can get the other half of the map out of the reef."

"There's a couple of tools I'll need to borrow from Joe," Steven said. "I'll get them tomorrow. Then I think we should plan to go to the pier the day after. That way, we can have one more day at the beach before vacation ends." He grinned and shook his head. "Won't old Joshua be surprised if we find that treasure?"

"If it's there, we'll find it," Jessica said confidently. Now that all three of them were in on the plan, they were bound to succeed. She darted another look at her twin. Elizabeth was frowning, looking as if she was lost in thought again.

Jessica quickly ran through all the elements of the story. Had Elizabeth told them everything?

Jessica didn't think so. Something about Elizabeth's face made Jessica wonder if she still had one or two ideas she was keeping to herself.

But she knew Elizabeth. When she had that look on her face, it meant she wasn't talking until she was good and ready.

After Elizabeth turned off the light and crawled into bed that night, she sat with her eyes wide open for a long time. Jessica had teased her about knowing more than she wanted to tell them, and she had been right. Elizabeth did have one more idea about the whole thing. But she wasn't ready to share it.

She could be wrong. But she didn't think she was.

The only thing about it was, if she told Steven and Jessica what she thought, they would think she had really gone over the edge.

"I'm going to have to do some research," she said out loud to the dark emptiness of her room.

Fifteen

◇

"Excuse me, Ms. Watkins," Elizabeth said in a low voice.

The librarian looked up and smiled. "Hi, there, Elizabeth. You're the first student I've seen in here all spring vacation. I sure am glad you came. I was beginning to think that being open on Sunday mornings was a waste of time."

The Sweet Valley Public Library had just instituted Sunday-morning hours as part of an effort to make the library more accessible to people who worked full-time. This branch of the library was just a few blocks from Elizabeth's house, and Elizabeth had always loved spending time there. It was quiet and pretty, and when the school library didn't have something, she could almost always count on Ms. Watkins to locate it for her.

Elizabeth smiled back at Ms. Watkins. "Well, I don't want you to think I'm a total nerd. I'm not here to do anything for school."

Ms. Watkins laughed. "So what can I help you with?"

Ms. Watkins was always interested in Elizabeth's projects. Unfortunately, Elizabeth didn't feel that she could explain what this project was all about. She hoped Ms. Watkins wouldn't ask her too many questions.

"Where would I look to find information about shipwrecks off the California coast?"

Ms. Watkins looked stumped for a moment. "Hmmmm. That's a good question. Any particular ship?"

Elizabeth bit her lip. If the ship had a name, she didn't know what it was. "I'm not sure. But I know the year of the wreck. Seventeen seventy-nine."

"Oh!" Ms. Watkins looked startled. "You really want some old information."

"I'm pretty sure there was a wreck on the reef just off Pirate's Cove in seventeen seventy-nine," Elizabeth explained. "The ship went down, and most of the passengers were lost. I was wondering if there might be any records anywhere that would list the names of the sailors who were on board." I just sort of got interested in some of the old beach lore of Sweet Valley."

Ms. Watkins nodded. "That kind of research project can become very absorbing," she agreed.

Elizabeth felt her shoulders relax. Ms. Watkins didn't seem to think her request for information was strange at all. That was good. It meant she wouldn't ask a lot of questions that Elizabeth didn't want to answer. And she sure wouldn't want to tell Ms. Watkins a lie.

The thoughtful frown on Ms. Watkins' face disappeared, and she snapped her fingers. "I know," she said in a satisfied voice. She picked up the telephone on her desk and began to dial. "I'm going to call Bill Dallas at the downtown branch. He's the archivist there. Maybe he'll have some ideas."

"Elizabeth!"

Elizabeth was on her way to the downtown branch of the library when she turned around and saw Amy Sutton standing on a corner and waving at her.

"Amy! What are you doing downtown?"

"My mom came downtown this morning to

shop. I'm supposed to meet her for lunch. Then we're both going to get our hair cut. I feel like I've been waiting forever, though. Do you know what time it is?"

Elizabeth looked at her watch. "It's ten past twelve."

Amy shrugged. "I guess I haven't been waiting that long. But it sure does feel like it. I guess because I'm standing up."

Elizabeth looked around and noticed for the first time that there were no benches in downtown Sweet Valley. "Benches," she said, suddenly getting an idea.

"Where?" Amy asked.

Elizabeth giggled. "Sorry. Didn't mean to get your hopes up. I was just thinking out loud. The town should put some benches around downtown so people can sit and rest. Or eat their lunch out of a paper bag."

"You're right," Amy agreed quickly. "And the sooner the better. My feet hurt."

Elizabeth's mind began racing. If they *did* find the map, and it *did* lead them to treasure, she would have a lot of money. Enough money to buy some benches for downtown.

Her eyes flew to the old bank building in the square. The clock had been broken for the last twenty years. It could only be repaired by clock-makers in Europe. The town of Sweet Valley had always felt they had more pressing needs for their public money, so they had never repaired the clock. But a clock that worked and chimed on the hour would do a lot for public morale. *I'll get the clock fixed*, she thought happily.

Suddenly, everywhere she looked, she saw things that could be repaired, restored, or refurbished. Wouldn't it be wonderful to be a fairy godmother to Sweet Valley? To grant all of its civic wishes? She could help fund the soup kitchen and rebuild the homeless shelter. She could fill the day-care center with new toys. . . . Suddenly she was as excited over the prospect of treasure as Steven and Jessica had been.

"Yoo-hoo, anybody home?" Amy asked, passing her hand in front of Elizabeth's eyes.

"Sorry," Elizabeth said with an embarrassed smile. "I was just . . . uh . . . having a little daydream."

"Hello, girls," said a familiar voice.

The girls turned and saw Mrs. Sutton coming down the street, carrying a large shopping bag.

"Hi, Mrs. Sutton," Elizabeth said.

Mrs. Sutton gave Elizabeth a little hug. "This is a nice surprise. Can you have lunch with us?"

"Come on," Amy immediately urged. "We're going to Forrester's, where they have all those fancy deserts."

"I'd better not," Elizabeth said regretfully. "I'm on my way to the library, and they're holding some materials for me."

"Going to the library during spring vacation?" Amy said. "What are you doing there?"

"Just a little independent research," Elizabeth answered evasively.

"Elizabeth!"

Good grief! It seemed that everybody in the world was downtown today.

Lila and Janet waved at her from the doorway of Bergman's Emporium, one of the most expensive department stores in Sweet Valley.

"What's up?" Elizabeth said with a smile, going over to join them.

"We're taking advantage of the spring sale," Janet answered.

"Speak for yourself," Lila said quickly. "I never buy things on sale." Her face got that snobby expression that Elizabeth knew so well. "The sale items always look so picked over and tattered."

Janet's face colored angrily, and Elizabeth had a hard time holding back a laugh. It was such a typical Lila remark. Half brag and half put-down. It was obvious from the size of her shopping bags that Janet had bought lots of sale items.

But Janet was just as snobby as Lila. And besides that, Lila was Janet's cousin. So instead of getting mad at Lila, she decided to take her anger out on Elizabeth. "Well, Elizabeth," she said in her Unicorn Club president voice, "I hope when school starts again in a few days you'll be too busy to put together any more chain-letter pranks."

"What?" Elizabeth demanded.

"That's right," Lila said. "Honestly. I can't believe the way you and Jessica managed to play such a mind game on me. I actually thought I heard a voice on a blank tape."

Lila and Janet exchanged a look and then shook their heads, as if they couldn't believe how immature Elizabeth was.

Elizabeth was furious. And inside her chest, there was a great struggle going on. If she wanted to, she could tell them a thing or two that would really scare them.

But then, why bother? It was better that they didn't believe it. This adventure wasn't big enough for everybody.

Elizabeth turned and began walking away.

"Hey!" Janet called out. "Where are you going?"

"The library," Elizabeth answered over her shoulder.

Suddenly, a feeling of excitement fluttered in her stomach. If they found the treasure, maybe that would shut Lila and Janet up once and for all.

Then Elizabeth felt immediately ashamed of herself. Wanting to have a lot of money just so she could make other people feel bad was the kind of thing Lila and Janet did.

"I don't want any treasure if it's going to change me into somebody I don't like," she blurted out loud.

A man passing by gave her a curious look.

Elizabeth blushed and then actually laughed out loud. The only thing dumber than counting chickens before they hatched was *worrying* about chickens before they hatched.

Mr. Dallas removed a large, heavy old book from a glass case and placed it carefully on top of the dark wood library table. "Seventeen seventy-nine, eh?"

"That's right," Elizabeth said.

Mr. Dallas reached into his pocket and took out a pair of white cotton gloves. He put them on before opening the old book. The leather covers were falling apart and the pages inside were old, yellowed, and practically disintegrating. "Probably no *complete* records if the ship went down. But there's always something left. A ship's log. A newspaper story. Letters from survivors. Something."

He turned the pages slowly and carefully. "Here's something," he said. "A newspaper account." He bent down to examine it. "Looks like this is your ship. A pardoned pirate and his noblewoman bride."

"That's it!" Elizabeth cried eagerly. "Is there a list of names? Names of the sailors on board?"

Mr. Dallas turned the page. "Here," he said, tapping the page with his finger. "Their names and their positions on the ship. A list of the survivors as well as the names of the men who were lost."

Elizabeth leaned over his arm. Her eyes flew down the list of unfamiliar names until finally, on the list of survivors, it rested on the one name she knew.

"Whoa!" Elizabeth shouted as a pair of strong arms shot out from behind the low hedge, wrapped around her, and pulled her through the tangled bushes into a front yard.

"Let go!" she shouted, starting to panic.

A hand came down on top of her head and pushed, forcing her to the ground. Another hand closed over her mouth, muffling her voice.

"Shhhh," she heard her attacker say. Then slowly, he removed her hand from her mouth.

She opened her eyes and saw . . .

"*Steven!*" she shouted angrily. "You almost scared me to—"

"Shhhh," he warned again, cutting her off. He cautiously lifted his head and peeped over the bushes. "Do you know that guy?" he whispered.

Elizabeth gingerly lifted her own head and peered over the bushes.

Coming around the same corner she had just turned on her way home from the library was John Filber.

"That's the guy that we met on the pier," she whispered. "The one whose family is cursed by Carlotta."

"Well, he's been following you since you got off the bus downtown," Steven whispered back.

"How do you know?"

"Because I've been following you, too," Steven responded with a grin. "All day."

"Why?"

"Because Jessica was worried about you."

"Jessica was worried about *me?*"

Steven put his hands to his lips. "Shhhh!" he warned again.

"Jessica was worried about *me?*" Elizabeth repeated in a whisper.

Steven nodded. "She thinks you're keeping something secret and that you're liable to go off on your own and get into trouble."

"Ha!" Elizabeth said in a fierce whisper. "Look who's talking. Jessica Wakefield thinks *I'm* going to get into trouble?"

Steven couldn't suppress a snort of laughter. "Come on," he said, signaling to her to keep her head down and follow him.

Together, they crept along the hedge until it reached the end of the block. Then they sprinted across the yard of one of their neighbors, turned sharply, climbed over the back fence, and came down in another neighbor's yard on the next street. From there, it was only a short walk to their own house.

"Now can we talk?" Elizabeth asked in a normal tone of voice.

Steven nodded.

"I'll bet that guy suspects something about

the map and the treasure," Elizabeth said.

"Well, duh," Steven responded dryly.

"But it doesn't matter, because he can't touch the map."

"You mean you really think he'd be cursed by Carlotta?"

"I don't think it," Elizabeth replied firmly. "I know it."

Sixteen

"I was at the library trying to get some information on the shipwreck," Elizabeth explained, sitting down on her brother's unmade bed.

Jessica and Steven exchanged a glance.

"Did you find out anything?" Jessica asked.

"Nothing I didn't already know," Elizabeth replied truthfully.

Jessica and Steven exchanged another glance. They had been grilling her ever since she and Steven came in the door.

They were sitting in Steven's room because it faced the front of the house. From time to time, one of them would get up to see if John Filber could be seen lurking outside anywhere. So far, he hadn't turned up.

"Promise you won't go off on your own again," Jessica said. "I mean, this whole thing is exciting. But it's scary, too. Especially now that we know that guy is following us."

"She's right," Steven said. "We've really got to stick together. Remember what Joshua told us on the first day. No straggling or going off on your own."

Elizabeth saluted. "Yes, sir."

"We'll move out tomorrow then, troops," he said with a grin.

"Tomorrow," the twins agreed.

Steven got up off of his bed and saluted as he left the room. "I'm going over to Joe's to see about some tools," he said. "I'll see you guys later."

By two o'clock that afternoon, Elizabeth's eyelids felt heavy as lead. "I need a nap," she announced.

Jessica looked up from her notebook and lifted her eyebrows in surprise. "Gee, Lizzie, you never take naps."

The two girls were sitting in the living room, listening to the radio and reading. Actually, Elizabeth was listening to the radio and reading. Jessica was making a list of all the things she planned to buy with her share of the treasure.

Elizabeth shook her head, trying to clear it. "I

know I don't. But I suddenly feel so sleepy I can hardly hold my head up."

"It's been a long few days," Jessica said. "I guess your body's trying to tell you something."

Elizabeth smiled. "I think I'll listen and go upstairs for a while."

Her feet felt even heavier than her eyelids as she trudged up the stairs. It was strange, this sleepy, drowsy feeling. But she couldn't fight it.

As soon as she was in her room, Elizabeth lay down on top of her bed and felt herself drifting off to sleep.

"Elizabeth!"

Elizabeth opened her eyes. It was so hard to see. She was surrounded by wet, heavy mist. So wet and so heavy, it was almost like being underwater.

"Elizabeth!" the voice cried again. "We're depending upon you."

"Carlottaaaaa . . . ," cried a man's voice from far away. "Carlottaaaaa. Where are you?"

Suddenly, from out of the mist, the tall beautiful woman appeared. She half floated, half swam in front of Elizabeth's gaze. Her long, dark hair flowed around her pale face like a halo.

"Carlotta!" Elizabeth gasped. But she felt no sense of fear. None at all.

Carlotta was holding out her hand. "Time grows short," she said in a voice throbbing with urgency. "All depends on you."

"Carlottaaaaa," the man's voice cried, breaking in despair. "Where are you? I've been searching for eternity."

"Help us," Carlotta begged. "Help us, Elizabeth."

"I will," Elizabeth promised. "I'll reunite you if I can. But please don't curse me if I can't do it."

"I? I curse you? Carlotta never cursed a soul."

"But what about the bosun?" Elizabeth cried. "You cursed him. And he can't rest. You cursed his descendants, too. That's why they can't touch the gold heart."

Carlotta shook her head. "No, child. The bosun cursed himself. His own conscience will not let him rest. Not until he has righted his wrong. His guilt is so deep, it survives the generations. That's the ill fortune that touches his descendants. Not any curse of my making."

"Then all along, it hasn't been you . . . it's been . . ."

"Carlottaaaaaaa . . . ," wailed the man's voice again, cutting Elizabeth off.

Carlotta turned, her long hair floating around her. "Time grows short," she repeated. "Shorter than you think. The night without stars is here. Help us. Reunite us."

"I will," Elizabeth cried, stepping forward. "But please, wait a moment. If you could just answer one more question I would . . ."

But the next thing she knew, Carlotta was gone.

"Carlotta!" Elizabeth called out.

There was no answer. Just deep, wet mist closing in on her again.

"CARLOTTA!" she yelled.

Elizabeth was swimming now, trying to find Carlotta. Her heart was breaking for the beautiful woman who had been separated from her true love for so long. And she wanted to promise again that she would do everything she could to put the lovers back together. She wanted to reassure her that she and Red Beard were not forgotten. And that she was their friend.

The next thing Elizabeth knew, someone was shaking her shoulders. Shaking her hard.

"Wake up," Jessica commanded.

Elizabeth opened her eyes. Her twin's face was just inches from her own.

"Wake up," Jessica repeated. "We've got trouble."

"What happened?" Elizabeth demanded, sitting up with a start.

Jessica walked over to the window and pulled back the curtain. "Look."

"Uh-oh," Elizabeth said, jumping to her feet. "When did this start?"

Outside, the blue sky had turned ominously gray and cloudy. Gusty winds were causing the trees outside to bend and sway. Clearly, a storm was moving in.

Is that why I was suddenly so sleepy? Elizabeth wondered. *Maybe Carlotta wanted to communicate with me. She knew the night without stars was going to be tonight. And she needed my help.*

"Where's Steven?" she asked. "We're going to have to get going right away."

Jessica pressed her face to the window. "Here he comes," she said eagerly. "And it looks like he's got a big bag of tools."

Elizabeth watched the sky through the bus window. Big black thunderheads were rushing in, turning the sky darker by the minute. There was a strange chill in the air. Trees whipped back and forth as gusts of wind shook their branches.

The three Wakefields, wearing their wetsuits over their bathing suits for warmth, sat in the very back of the bus as it hurtled through the streets of Sweet Valley toward the north end of the beach.

Crash! Bam!

Elizabeth jumped at the sound.

"What was that?" Jessica asked breathlessly.

She squinted out the window and let out a sigh of relief. "Just some metal garbage cans. The wind blew them over and they rolled out into the street."

Jessica breathed a sigh of relief. "I was afraid it was lightning."

"If there's lightning, we can't get near the water," Steven said to his sisters. "No arguments about that, OK?"

"Let's not even say the word *lightning*," Jessica said. "It might jinx us."

Steven nodded. "OK by me. From now on, nobody's allowed to say it."

Elizabeth nodded. They were taking a big chance going out on the water in weather like this. But Jessica and Steven were as determined as she was to see the mystery through to the end. Their reasons were different, though.

Jessica and Steven were looking forward to finding a treasure. Elizabeth would be happy about that, too, of course, but now, after being visited by Carlotta, what she really wanted to do was reunite the lovers and end their long, heart-breaking separation.

"Anybody following us?" Steven asked, turning around to look through the back window of the bus.

"Too dark to tell," Jessica replied, turning in her seat.

The weather had turned the sky so dark that cars on the road had their lights on. Traffic was heavy, but it was impossible to tell if any one car was sticking close to the bus.

"Everybody keep an eye out when we get off the bus," Steven said.

Elizabeth felt a little chill of fear skate up her spine.

"Brrrrr," Jessica said, giving a little nervous shiver. "This is exciting but nerve-racking."

Steven hoisted his pack up into his lap and began checking through his tools. "Don't get rattled. We know what we have to do and we're totally prepared." He gave the pack a little shake, and it gave a reassuring clank. "Two flashlights," he said proudly. "Rope. Pick. Hammer and chisel."

"Got the heart?" Jessica asked suddenly, a note of panic in her voice.

Elizabeth tapped the neck of her wetsuit. "On a chain around my neck and tucked down into the suit."

Steven and Jessica grinned.

In spite of her nervousness, Elizabeth grinned, too. This was one of the most exciting things that had ever happened to her in her whole life, and she was glad to be sharing it with Jessica and Steven.

Seventeen

"Hurry," Steven urged, over the sound of the swirling, whistling wind.

Jessica's hair whipped back and forth across her face. She brushed it roughly back and took her hand off the rope so she could tuck it into her wetsuit.

"Keep twisting!" Elizabeth commanded.

Immediately, Jessica put her hands back on the rope.

They were rigging up a safety harness for Steven, twisting the rope around one of the heavy pilings along the pier.

"One or two more turns and that ought to do it," Steven said, tying the other end of the rope firmly around his waist. "I can't believe it," he shouted gleefully over the wind. "A map on the back of a locket. We're going to find that treasure."

Jessica sneaked a peek up at the sky. It was almost black now, but the rain was still holding off. And thankfully, there was no lightning. Not yet.

Suddenly, her hands began to shake with excitement. Soon they were going to be holding both halves of a treasure map. She began picturing a big trunk full of diamonds and doubloons and gold jewelry. They'd all get their pictures in the paper. And Elizabeth could write a whole big article for the Sunday Supplement about it.

And maybe somebody would buy the rights to their story and make a movie out of it. And maybe she would even get to star in it and—

"Jessica!" Elizabeth said, interrupting her thoughts. "Did you hear me?"

"Huh?" Jessica asked with a nervous grin.

"Steven said to hand him the pack."

Jessica reached behind her, grabbed Steven's pack, and handed it over. She noticed that Elizabeth's face looked really tense. So did Steven's. "You two aren't going to chicken out, are you?" she asked suddenly.

"Not me," Steven said immediately, pulling a heavy hammer and chisel from the pack.

"Not me either," Elizabeth said. "I feel like I have sort of a personal commitment to see this thing through."

"Come on. Let's move," Steven said as he looked up at the sky. "It's getting darker by the minute, and when the rain starts, we're going to have a hard time."

The girls both grabbed the rope and held it tightly while Steven lowered himself over the side of the pier.

"Watch out for the undertow," Jessica shouted. "It's really strong around the jetty posts."

Steven nodded and picked his way gracefully along the pieces of coral reef that stuck up through the water. "I'm going to stay out of the water altogether if I can," he answered. "Whoaaa!" he yelled as his foot slipped out from underneath him and he fell.

Jessica and Elizabeth pulled on the rope, hoisting him back to his feet, and he again balanced himself on the coral reef. "OK?" Jessica shouted in a worried tone.

"OK," he assured them.

The girls watched breathlessly as he made his way to the coral face where the little piece of gold winked through the foggy afternoon. Steven squatted down, positioned the chisel, and then brought the hammer down on top of it.

Bang!

Little pieces of coral flew in all directions.

"Careful," Elizabeth warned. "You don't want to break it out and knock it into the water.

Steven nodded his head. Then he lifted the hammer again. This time he brought it down more gently.

Jessica let her breath out. It was going to work. It was really going to work.

Elizabeth was practically shuddering with the suspense. Steven had been chipping at the coral for over fifteen minutes. Chipping softly and carefully, trying to dislodge the piece of metal that they were sure was the other half of the heart.

"I think this is it," Steven said in an odd, strangled voice.

Elizabeth felt her breath catch in her chest. Her hands flew to her neck, making sure the half she wore there was still safely in place.

Steven brought the hammer down, and from where Elizabeth stood she could see the coral break up into rubble just under Steven's hand.

Very carefully, he brushed away the bits and pieces and then he let out a loud shout of triumph. *"Got it!"* he yelled, lifting his fist. "We're gonna be rich!"

Immediately, Jessica and Elizabeth began pulling on the rope. Elizabeth's legs were shaking so much, she could hardly stand.

Finally, after what seemed like hours, Steven had navigated the slippery climb back up on the pier. He stood in front of them holding half of a gold heart in his hand.

It was dented a little. And it was nicked on the edge. But it was all there.

"Look on the back," Jessica said in a hoarse whisper.

Steven turned it over. "The other half of the map," he breathed.

Elizabeth immediately removed the other half from around her neck and held it out for Steven.

"Hold it!" a voice shouted out of nowhere.

Jessica let out a little shriek. Elizabeth was so badly startled, she almost dropped her half of the heart.

The three of them whirled around.

"You!" Elizabeth cried, her heart pounding against her rib cage.

John Filber stood a few yards behind them, a stony expression on his face. "I was here waiting," he said. "Under the pier." He nodded to

Elizabeth. "I heard everything you said. Today, after you came out of the library, I went in and asked a few questions, too. Got the same information you did about the ship. About the pirate. And about Carlotta. I grew up on all those old sea stories. Stories about a treasure and a map engraved on a heart. But I never knew what was true and what wasn't. Now I do." His tone was gruff and threatening. "Hand over the map."

Elizabeth stared at him, stunned.

"Give it to him," Steven said quickly. He held out his hand to give John Filber the heart.

But quick as lightning, Elizabeth's hand shot out, grabbed it, and held Steven's half of the locket against her own. The two pieces of the heart fit together seamlessly to form one perfect heart. She gasped as it seemed to grow warm suddenly in her palm, almost as if it were alive and beating. She felt as if she were holding Carlotta's and Red Beard's hearts, and their destinies, in her hand.

"Give it to me!" John Filber said nastily. He took a threatening step forward.

Elizabeth took a deep breath and opened her palm. Let John Filber have the map. Let him have the treasure. The important thing was that Red

Beard and Carlotta were together. Reunited at last.

"Here," she said, holding her hand out to John Filber. "Take it."

John Filber hurried forward and snatched at the heart.

His guilt is so deep, it survives the generations, Carlotta had said.

Now they would see if the family curse was real or not.

"Thanks for making me a rich man," John Filber said with an vicious laugh. He grabbed the heart from Elizabeth's hand and then turned and began running down the pier. Just as he reached the section that led to the beach, there was a tremendous clap of thunder and a bolt of lightning streaked across the sky. Waves kicked up from the surging sea rolled over the pier.

John Filber yelled as he lost his footing and fell heavily.

"Oh, no!" Jessica shrieked.

They watched in horror as something small and golden rolled across the pier and fell into the churning sea.

Hand in hand, the three Wakefields ran toward the safety of the covered bus stop, leaving behind them John Filber, the gold heart, and the churning sea.

Elizabeth cast one final look over her shoulder.

Far away, down the beach, she thought she saw a solitary figure continue walking until he disappeared into the mist and the driving rain.

"Are you kidding?" Jessica shrieked. "Joshua Farrell is *not* a ghost!"

Elizabeth bit her lip in frustration. "But I—but how else do you—"

"Oh, come on," Steven said. "I know this whole thing's been pretty unbelievable. But that's so unbelievably unbelievable, I can't believe it."

It was seven o'clock and the three of them were dry, showered, and sitting around the kitchen table drinking hot chocolate and eating a huge bowl of buttered popcorn.

Elizabeth popped two big fluffy kernels into her mouth. "Joshua Farrell was the name of the bosun who left his post so he could look for Red Beard's treasure map just before the ship was wrecked in 1779. The wreck was his fault. He survived that wreck. And he must have married and had children. But maybe when he died, his spirit couldn't rest. He felt too guilty about what he had done to Red Beard and Carlotta. I mean, I realize that sounds pretty crazy. But I can't figure out another way to explain it."

"So you're saying the curse of Carlotta was really the curse of Joshua Farrell?"

"That's right," Elizabeth said. "All the letters and dreams and spooky things that happened were caused by Joshua, not by Carlotta."

"I'm still confused," Steven said.

"Joshua was wandering Pirate's Cove the day I found the first half of the heart. He saw me get out of the water, heard Carlotta's voice on the wind, and saw the way the sea was behaving. So he knew. He knew I must have found half of the heart. And I guess finally, after two hundred years, he saw a way to put things right."

"So he sent us the chain letters," Jessica said.

"That's right. We thought it was Carlotta casting a wide net to search for the other half. But it was Joshua. He knew the other half had to be somewhere, and the chain letter led us to it."

"By way of John Filber," Steven said.

Elizabeth nodded. "That's right."

"Why all the tricks?" Jessica asked. "Why the empty wetsuit and the faceless mask?"

"I guess to scare me," Elizabeth said. "To make me take all the spooky stuff seriously. So I would cooperate."

"Well, it sure was an elaborate scheme," Steven said skeptically. Then he snorted. "Lizzie, I think we've all been the victims of brain fever or something. Do you realize what an unbelievable thing we're believing?"

Elizabeth wiggled her toes contentedly inside her warm fuzzy slippers. Now that they were safe and warm inside the Wakefields' cozy kitchen, it *was* hard to believe any of it had happened.

She noticed Steven giving her an odd glance. "You know, Lizzie," he said in a slow, thoughtful voice, "nobody saw any of the strange stuff but you."

Jessica reached for some popcorn and her hand froze in midair as if she had just had a sudden thought. "Nobody saw *anything* but you," she said.

Elizabeth sat back in her chair and let her mouth fall open. "But I told you . . ."

"That's right," Steven said with a grin. "You told us. *You told* us about the dreams. *You told* us about the empty wetsuit. *You told* us everything."

"But you both saw the letters."

"That's right," Jessica said. "We did see the letters."

Steven smiled knowingly. "I also saw you take a calligraphy course last summer."

Jessica's mouth fell open and she let out a little indignant scream. "That's right!" she yipped. "*You* wrote those letters. Elizabeth Wakefield, how dare you pull such a big hoax on us. On *me*?"

"It wasn't a hoax," Elizabeth protested, her voice rising. "What about John Filber and—"

"Yeah, I guess John Filber came as a big surprise," Steven said, choking back a laugh. "And I'll bet it came as a big surprise to find out there really was a heart all along. You based this joke on an old Pirate's Cove legend, and the legend turned out to be true. But as far as the rest of it goes, the supernatural stuff, the treasure and all that . . ." Steven shook his head. "I'm just coming up with too many rational explanations."

"She got us," Jessica said.

"She got us good," Steven agreed.

Jessica and Steven were convulsed in laughter now. "Boy. You really had us going there," Steven said, wheezing. He was bent practically double. "If it weren't so funny, I'd be mad."

"I *am* mad," Jessica joked, picking up a handful of popcorn and pelting Elizabeth with it.

"That's the spirit," Steven shouted.

The next thing she knew, Elizabeth was being

pelted with popcorn by both Steven and Jessica.

Under the circumstances, there was only one thing to do. Pelt them back.

Elizabeth grabbed a handful of popcorn, let out a yell, and then let them have it.

Elizabeth snuggled under the covers that night feeling warm and happy. She was more relaxed than she'd felt all spring vacation. She was even a little bit excited about going back to school.

So what if Steven and Jessica didn't believe in ghosts or curses or Carlotta and Red Beard? Now that everything was back to normal, she wasn't so sure what she herself believed anymore.

All she knew was that she was going to get a good, long sleep that night, without shipwrecks or ghosts or terrible storms.

Counting backward from one hundred, Elizabeth floated into a deep sleep. . . .

She was sitting on the end of the pier at Pirate's Cove. The sky was turning an inky black as storm clouds raced overhead. Suddenly, a bolt of lightning seemed to split the sky, and rain began to pour down. It pounded the pier and drenched Elizabeth. She felt the cold damp wind on her face. The sea was boiling and churning.

Over the roar of the waves, the crashing thunder, and the pounding rain, Elizabeth heard the terrible, chilling moan. Carlotta's moan. Elizabeth felt her body clench with fear as a steamy, thick mist began rolling in from the sea.

Suddenly she saw something emerge from the mist. It was vague at first, almost transparent, but slowly she made out the prow of a great ship. The pirate ship!

And at that instant, the mist parted and she saw the most wonderful sight in the world: Carlotta and Red Beard standing on the prow of the ship locked in a passionate embrace. Carlotta's long, dark hair framed her pale, beautiful face and hung down over her deep pink velvet gown.

As Elizabeth looked into Carlotta's and Red Beard's faces, she felt a sense of relief flow over her. Their faces were filled with joy, and Elizabeth knew in her heart that they'd never be separated again.

Carlotta looked up, and for a moment her eyes met Elizabeth's. She smiled, and Elizabeth knew it was a smile of thanks.

Miraculously, the sky began to clear. The rain stopped, the sky grew still and quiet, and the thick mist began to evaporate.

Elizabeth watched with a full heart as Carlotta and Red Beard sailed away into the clear morning sunlight.

SIGN UP FOR THE SWEET VALLEY HIGH® FAN CLUB!

Hey, girls! Get all the gossip on Sweet Valley High's® most popular teenagers when you join our fantastic Fan Club! As a member, you'll get all of this really cool stuff:

- Membership Card with your own personal Fan Club ID number
- A Sweet Valley High® Secret Treasure Box
- Sweet Valley High® Stationery
- Official Fan Club Pencil (for secret note writing!)
- Three Bookmarks
- A "Members Only" Door Hanger
- Two Skeins of J. & P. Coats® Embroidery Floss with flower barrette instruction leaflet
- Two editions of *The Oracle* newsletter
- Plus exclusive Sweet Valley High® product offers, special savings, contests, and much more!

Be the first to find out what Jessica & Elizabeth Wakefield are up to by joining the Sweet Valley High® Fan Club for the one-year membership fee of only $6.25 each for U.S. residents, $8.25 for Canadian residents (U.S. currency). Includes shipping & handling.

Send a check or money order (do not send cash) made payable to "Sweet Valley High® Fan Club" along with this form to:

SWEET VALLEY HIGH® FAN CLUB, BOX 3919-B, SCHAUMBURG, IL 60168-3919

NAME_____
(Please print clearly)

ADDRESS_____

CITY_____ STATE _____ ZIP_____
(Required)

AGE_____ BIRTHDAY_____ /_____ /_____

Offer good while supplies last. Allow 6-8 weeks after check clearance for delivery. Addresses without ZIP codes cannot be honored. Offer good in USA & Canada only. Void where prohibited by law.
©1993 by Francine Pascal   LCI-1383-123